Love at VARGAS
RANCH BOOK 1

HER
Mistaken
IDENTITY
Cowboy

KAREN BANEY

desert life
media

Her Mistaken Identity Cowboy (Love at Vargas Ranch Book 1)
By Karen Baney

Publisher:
Desert Life Media, LLC
Gilbert, AZ 85295

www.karenbaney.com

Printed in the United States of America

ISBN-978-1-960217-71-4

And be kind and compassionate to one another,
forgiving one another,
just as God also forgave you in Christ.
— Ephesians 4:32 CSB

Foreword

WELCOME TO VARGAS Ranch!

If you've read my original *Vargas Ranch Series*, you already know the Vargas family and their beloved Arizona guest ranch. You've met Dalton, Dylan, Derin, Devon, Drake, Solana, and Renata. You've watched them fall in love, find faith, and build their futures.

But what about everyone else at the ranch?

The *Love at Vargas Ranch Series* tells the love stories of the cowboys, wranglers, and staff who make Vargas Ranch come alive. These are the people working behind the scenes—leading trail rides, managing the equine therapy program, running the sports complex, and keeping ranch operations running smoothly. Their stories unfold alongside the Vargas family's journey, filling in the moments between the books you've already loved.

For those of you discovering my books for the first time—welcome! While the *Love at Vargas Ranch* books connect to my original series, each story stands completely on its own. You won't miss a single beat starting here with Parker and Shannon's story. You'll meet the Vargas family as the owners of the ranch where Shannon and Parker are building their new lives.

Whether you're returning to Vargas Ranch or visiting for the first time, I'm thrilled to share these stories of faith, healing, and love under the Arizona desert sky.

Happy reading!

Karen Baney

1

———

ALL THE STEREOTYPES about identical twins finishing each other's sentences and being besties for life—those were lies. Parker Quaid knew it firsthand.

He jammed his cell phone into his pocket, frowning so deeply he could almost feel his eyebrows touching. His twin had struck again.

"Parker!"

He turned toward the sound of his boss, Dylan Vargas' voice, cutting through the low murmur of morning activity in the barn.

"C-c-could you get Pansy and Red ready?"

"Sure thing."

Parker had been hired on at Vargas Ranch for all of two months. He liked it here. The wide-open desert. Sunrises painted in soft gold and burnt orange, stretching endlessly over the horizon. The quiet, still mornings with room for a man to think. Maybe too much room.

For the first time in years, nobody here knew his name was connected to headlines about fraud or theft. The Vargas family had hired him based on his experience with horses, not his brother's reputation. Dylan and Adan treated him like any other ranch hand, with respect earned through honest work. If that changed, if they started looking at him the way everyone else eventually did, he'd have nowhere left to go.

He ambled toward Pansy's stall, the horse whuffling softly, her breath warm as he stepped inside. The smell of hay and leather filled the air, earthy and familiar. He placed the halter carefully over her head, opened the gate, and led her down the alleyway to the grooming area, hooves clopping against the packed dirt with a steady rhythm.

Routine. He liked routine. It didn't ask questions or cast suspicion. Didn't look at him sideways like he might turn crooked any minute, just because his twin had.

He ran the brush along Pansy's coat, slow and steady, the soft scrape of bristles blending with the distant creak of a stall door swinging shut. His mind drifted to the email waiting for him from his attorney. Bad news. He already knew it. He hadn't even needed to read past the first line.

Lucas had conned an elderly widow out of thousands of dollars, promising her a fake land deal, taking her retirement savings, and then vanishing. Parker barely knew this latest victim, but she reminded him of Mrs. Chen, another widow Lucas had targeted back in Flagstaff. Mrs. Chen had looked at Parker afterward like he was pure evil, unable to see past his identical face to recognize that he'd tried to warn her. The memory still made his stomach turn. And somehow, through forged documents and slick talking, Lucas had done it again. He'd gained another woman's trust just to destroy her life.

This time, he'd used Parker's social security number when the court ruled against him, forcing Parker to pay reparations. He snorted, the sound abrupt in the still air. Like Lucas would ever work an honest day in his life.

The injustice of it all made Parker tighten the saddle's cinch harder than necessary. Pansy shifted away from him, her tail flicking in irritation. He exhaled slowly, rubbing his hand along her neck in silent apology. None of this was her fault. It wasn't even entirely his own. But that hadn't mattered to his previous employer, who put more weight on the court's ruling tied to his social than the name on the judgment being different. They'd garnished his wages and sent the money to the court for distribution.

Parker quit when he found out. His attorney was still trying to straighten it all out. The email didn't look promising. He might not get a dime of it back.

The Vargases had given him a chance when no one else would. If they saw him as just another Quaid disaster, he'd lose more than a job. He'd lose the only place that still felt like his.

The old fable about Midas? Lucas was the opposite. Everything he touched burned.

Parker led Pansy to the trail ride staging area, tying her off at the rail. The packed dirt smelled faintly of mesquite and sunbaked silt, a far cry from the crisp chill of Flagstaff.

As he passed Adan Franco on the way back down the alleyway, the ranch hand tipped his hat in greeting, boots scuffing against the ground.

His mind started recounting all the ways Lucas's crimes had made his life difficult as he brushed Red's coat. Parker had been arrested no less than five times. That's how he learned odd little facts about identical twins, like that their fingerprints were different. Bless the one cop in Flagstaff who told him about it. Saved him from actually going to jail or serving prison time for his twin.

He shook his head. Didn't do him any good dwelling on things he couldn't control. Adan would tell him not to count the offenses. Sage advice.

Parker finished readying Red before leading him out to the staging area. Dylan thanked him before giving a few parting instructions and mounting up.

He watched as the group rode away, a smile twitching at the corner of his mouth when a teenage girl squealed. Something about her horse going too fast. It wasn't. Barely a walk. Clearly a novice.

Turning on his booted heel, he dragged the large barn

door closed, the track groaning in protest. Despite it being November, the temperatures were still climbing up to the low-nineties. A little unseasonably warm for the Sonoran desert. Dust swirled lazily in the air, catching in the faint breeze.

Back home, it probably would have snowed by now. Crisp, chilly mountain air. Fresh. None of this dust-laden stuff.

He growled in frustration. He needed to pull himself out of his foul mood. Lucas won only if Parker gave in to bitterness. He knew that, but letting go wasn't easy.

Toasted Toffee was due for time in the corral, so Parker led the ranch manager's horse out for some fresh air and exercise before returning inside.

He stowed the extra saddle pads in the dimly lit tack room, the familiar scent of saddle soap and worn leather filling the space. Then he hosed down the grooming area, listening to the steady rush of water hitting the textured concrete floor.

Finally, he stepped into the office to check the schedule.

Only to run into the most beautiful woman. Warm chocolate brown eyes. Long brown hair.

He steadied her, her floral-scented shampoo lingering in the space between them, warmth sparking under his skin. Her rounded eyes settled for a beat or two into something almost apologetic.

Then, as if this day hadn't been bad enough, her eyes lit with fire that could scorch the earth.

"You!"

Parker's shoulders tensed automatically, muscle memory from too many confrontations just like this one. His hands twitched toward his sides in the same unconscious movement he'd developed after being cuffed so many times. The familiar dread settled in his gut like a stone.

Knowing full well he'd never met the woman before in his life, Parker could only assume Lucas had struck again.

He could see it in the way her breathing had gone shallow and quick, how her hands trembled despite her fierce grip on whatever righteous anger was driving her forward. This wasn't just recognition. This was someone whose life Lucas had torn apart, and now she was staring at his face again. Parker's chest tightened with something that might have been sympathy, if he wasn't about to pay the price for his brother's crimes all over again.

———

SHANNON BURKE OWED everything to her great-aunt. So when Shirley had called three weeks ago with excitement bubbling in her voice, Shannon had listened carefully.

"There's a family here in Wickenburg doing something extraordinary," Aunt Shirley had said, her words crisp with the diction that had served as a voice coach for Hollywood's elite for decades. "Dylan Vargas—you remember him? He's the young man I work with on his speech therapy. He and his best friend are starting an equine therapy program for disabled children and veterans."

A familiar flutter of possibility had stirred in her heart, the same sensation she'd experienced six years ago when Aunt Shirley had first described her vision for helping people with speech impediments.

"They're looking for someone with nonprofit expertise to launch and run the organization," Aunt Shirley had continued. "I immediately thought of you."

For the past six years, Shannon had poured herself into building Aunt Shirley's organization from a passionate dream into a thriving operation. She'd developed systems, trained leaders, created sustainable funding streams, and, most importantly, watched her great-aunt's vision transform hundreds of lives. Now that foundation was solid, running smoothly under the capable leadership Shannon had cultivated. The work that had once challenged every skill she possessed had become routine.

The conversation with Aunt Shirley had lasted two hours, filled with details about their vision and Adan's nephew Braden—a four-year-old double amputee who'd discovered his love for horses despite his prosthetics. By the end of the call, Shannon's mind was already racing with possibilities.

An equine therapy charity for disabled children and veterans. The cause spoke to her heart in ways that went beyond career goals. She could visualize the entire plan, from the careful program development to introducing the charity to the local philanthropic community. And the Christmas gala, a December fundraiser, to launch them into the public consciousness with elegance and impact.

She'd spent the past three weeks researching, planning, and dreaming. This was the chance to build something meaningful from its very foundation, to take every lesson she'd learned from her success and apply it to an even more personal mission.

Shannon checked the time as she pulled into the parking lot of Vargas Ranch. The guest ranch manager had said Dylan and Adan were out on a trail ride with guests, but they should be back soon.

She stepped out into the warm November air, the soft scent of mesquite and sun-drenched earth drifting toward her. The desert landscape stretched in all directions, dotted with saguaro cacti standing proud like guardians of the hope blooming here. In the distance, purple mountains rose from the horizon, their peaks touched with the golden light of late afternoon.

As she walked across the grounds, Shannon took in the lush desert landscaping clearly designed with both beauty and practicality in mind. Palo Verde trees with their distinctive green trunks provided shade along the pathways. Texas sage bushes displayed their thick silvery leaves as a backdrop for the golden lantana mounds edging the gravel pathways.

It was beautiful. Peaceful. The perfect setting where God could cultivate healing in body, mind, and soul.

A blur of movement caught her attention. Broad shoulders. A man's purposeful stride disappeared around the corner of the main stable building.

Something about the man nagged at her. The way he moved. The tilt of his head.

She pushed the thought away. Just nerves about the interview.

Shannon opened the side door, and warm air rolled over her, followed by the smells of hay, worn leather, and horses. As she stepped into the dim corridor, something tightened in her chest.

The stable stretched longer than she'd expected, stalls lining both sides. A low nicker drifted from somewhere ahead. The soft shuffle of hooves against straw. The metallic clink of a halter against a stall door.

She called out a greeting.

Only the horses answered.

Shannon moved deeper into the building, her heels clicking against the textured concrete. Past curious equine faces turning to watch her progress. Past equipment rooms branching off the main alleyway. The office must be near the tack room, she reasoned, continuing forward, mind still stuck on the man she'd seen.

That walk. That exact tilt of his head.

Eight years vanished in a blink. She was back on NAU's campus, shaken and twenty and wrecked.

Her stomach dropped.

No, it couldn't be.

She rounded the corner near the tack room and collided straight into a wall of solid muscle.

Shannon gasped, stumbling backward. Firm hands shot out to steady her. The scent of clean sweat and worn leather filled her senses. The contact sent shock waves through her system, and then ice flooded her veins as her gaze traveled upward.

Everything went still.

Lucas Quaid.

The world spun off its axis. She was twenty again, staring at bank statements that made no sense, sitting in administrators' offices while they looked at her like she was criminally stupid or willfully complicit.

Her throat constricted. This man had stolen everything from her. Not just her money or her ability to finish college without crushing debt, but her ability to trust her own judgment.

The sharp jawline. The piercing blue eyes. Every detail exactly the same.

Her body reacted before conscious thought caught up. A jerky step backward, shoulders snapping into defensive position. Heart slamming against her ribs.

"Y-you," she stammered, voice tight and strangled. "I don't know how..."

The words wouldn't come. Not past the roar building in her ears, not through the cascade of memories crashing over her like a flash flood—devastating, unstoppable, sweeping away everything she'd built to protect herself.

He was right here.

After eight years. After everything he'd done.

Her phone. She needed her phone.

Shannon snatched it from her pocket with shaky fingers, nearly dropping it. Her trembling hands fumbled across the screen. The Maricopa County Sheriff's Office.

The line rang once. Twice.

When the dispatcher answered, Shannon's voice came out hard and sharp, cutting through the thick air between them.

"This is Shannon Burke. I'm at Vargas Ranch in Wickenburg. You need to send deputies immediately." Her eyes locked on Lucas with laser intensity, her grip so tight around the phone that her knuckles went white.

"Lucas Quaid is here, and I want him arrested."

2

———————

PARKER DREW IN a ragged breath, his gut clenching so tight he thought it might shrivel up. Not again. This woman, whoever she was, thought he was Lucas. And she was about to have him arrested. Again.

His pulse jolted, frustration coiling like a whip inside his chest. He lifted his hands slowly and measured, knowing full well how this could go sideways real fast. Had before.

"Hold up," he said, voice clipped. "I don't know what Lucas did to you, but I promise you. I'm not him."

Her glare cut through him like a blade, unyielding.

"I'm his identical twin."

She scoffed, a bitter, flat-out disbelieving sound. "How convenient."

Parker's jaw locked as he exhaled through his nose. He pointed to the small scar above his eyebrow, trying one last time. "Lucas ever have this?" he pressed, keeping his tone firm but restrained.

Her eyes flicked up just for a fraction of a second with a moment of uncertainty. That brief hesitation told him everything. She knew Lucas well enough to know the difference.

Her fingers tightened around her phone. She was still making the call.

He moved for his wallet, ready to yank out his driver's license even if it wouldn't prove much to someone half-crazed with fury. The glint of metal stopped him cold.

Mace. She had mace.

He froze, hands up again, heat burning through his chest. "Do not use that in the stables," he bit out. "You'll spook the horses."

Her laugh was bitter, hollow. "You should have been concerned for me," she snapped, voice shaking with rage deeper than anger. "For my life. For what stealing my college fund did to me."

Parker's stomach plummeted. Not because she was still aiming the mace straight at his face, but because he could hear it. The wounds, the betrayal, the sheer weight of what Lucas had done to her. She wasn't just angry. She was wrecked.

And before he could even attempt another word, boots thudded against the dirt outside. Voices carried on the breeze. The ranch hands were back.

Parker had never been more grateful to hear Dylan's deep voice and Adan's easygoing chatter. They rounded the corner, and all conversation stopped. The moment froze. Tension solidified in the air, hanging so thick Parker could practically feel Dylan's frown from ten feet away.

Adan lifted both hands, attempting to calm the situation. "Ma'am," Adan started, his tone lined with caution, "let's take a breath, yeah?"

Shannon didn't budge, didn't drop the mace, her chest rising and falling fast. "He's Lucas Quaid," she spat out, voice tight, shaking, pointing at Parker like he was the devil himself.

Parker shook his head emphatically. "No. I. Am. Not."

Adan stepped forward, cutting through the tension, using that smooth, unflappable tone he was known for. "All right, let's just talk about this outside," Adan said carefully, as if Shannon might crack at any moment.

A long, excruciating beat. Then she dropped her arm. Not fully. But enough.

Parker didn't dare move. Adan gestured toward the door, guiding her out slowly, like she was a spooked horse that might bolt at any second.

The crunch of tires on gravel sent heat crawling up Parker's spine. The deputies had arrived. And the second they stepped inside, the energy in the room shifted. Heavy, authoritative, like judgment had already been passed before a single word was spoken.

The lead deputy, a broad, no-nonsense guy with an unflinching gaze, didn't waste time. "You're Lucas Quaid?"

Parker's jaw tightened so hard it ached. "No." He forced out the word, even and controlled because he already knew where this was going. "I'm his twin. Identical twin."

The deputy's stare didn't flicker. "ID."

Parker exhaled through his nose, fingers itching to shove his hands deep in his pockets, but he kept them where they were. Visible, calm, cooperative. He pulled out his wallet, flipping it open to his driver's license, handing it over.

A pause. Too long. And then a flicker of doubt passed over the deputy's face.

"That's the right last name," the deputy muttered, turning the ID toward his partner. "But it's not the first one on all these warrants."

Parker's stomach dropped. Shannon made a choked sound, like she couldn't believe this was even up for debate.

"That's because he's lying!" she yelled, voice tight. "That's Lucas Quaid, and you need to take him in right now."

Parker shook his head, anger rising to the surface. "For the last time, I am not Lucas."

The lead deputy's expression didn't change. "This ID alone doesn't prove anything," he said, calmly, coldly.

Parker's pulse spiked. They weren't going to let him go. This was happening again. Again, because of Lucas. Because of his brother's crimes, his brother's face, his brother's carnage that had followed him his entire life.

And he should have kept his mouth shut. Should have just endured it silently—turning the other cheek—and let them drag him down to the station like they always did. But the rage inside him flashed.

His gut twisted, his voice edged with barely suppressed fury. "I told you I'm not him!" The words lashed out, his frustration boiling over despite every warning in his head telling him to stay controlled.

The deputy didn't flinch. But his partner moved lightning-fast.

The hard click of cuffs locked around Parker's wrists. His face smashed against the nearest stall, cowboy hat tumbling to the alley floor before he could even process the shift. His muscles went rigid as anger coursed under his skin. And then the sudden jerk as they yanked him forward, toward the cruiser, dragging him out into the harsh glare of the sun.

Shannon stood stone-still, her expression unreadable. She had done this. Lucas had done this. And Parker? Parker was going to pay for it anyway.

The sharp bite of cold metal against his wrists was nothing new. Didn't make it any less infuriating.

The cruiser door slammed shut, trapping him inside the cramped backseat. The faint scent of old vinyl, stale sweat, and dust hung in the air as the deputies climbed in, their voices low, murmuring things he didn't care to hear. None of it would change the fact that he was stuck in this nightmare again.

Parker sat rigid, shoulders pressed against the seat. His hands grew numb, trapped between his back and the seat as the cuffs dug into his wrists. Shannon Burke. The name meant nothing to him, but the fire in her eyes, the rage in her voice, the way she'd spat every word like a weapon. Lucas had destroyed her life. And she was determined to make sure he paid for it.

Except she had the wrong Quaid.

Parker's jaw ticked, frustration boring deep into his ribs.

Outside the cruiser, the deputies exchanged a few clipped sentences before pulling away from Vargas Ranch, the gravel lot kicking up dust.

The cruiser rumbled down the road, every bump jarring through Parker's spine, the cuffs digging into his wrists. He kept his gaze fixed out the window, watching the desert landscape blur by, trying and failing to unclench his jaw.

He wasn't new to this. Had been dragged in before. Always the same story. Somebody caught Lucas pulling one of his scams, then saw Parker. And suddenly, he was the prime suspect.

The heat of the sun burned against the window, but his gut was colder than steel. They pulled into the parking lot, tires crunching on asphalt. And then Shannon's car rolled in behind them.

Parker stared straight ahead as tension coiled between his shoulder blades. Of course she'd come. She wasn't done with him yet.

As soon as the cruiser door opened, he was yanked forward, boots skidding slightly on the pavement before the deputy steadied him with a firm grip. Inside, the office was cool, punctuated by the rhythmic clacking of keyboards and muffled phone conversations.

The lead deputy, Long according to his name tag, nudged Parker toward the front desk, flipping open a stack of files, expression unreadable. "Let's start," the deputy said, glancing up. "You claim you're not Lucas Quaid."

Parker gritted his teeth. "Because I'm not."

Deputy Long slid his ID across the desk. "We've got dozens of active warrants under the name 'Lucas Quaid.' You want us to believe this ID proves otherwise?"

Parker swallowed the irritation crawling through his chest. "This ID proves my legal name is Parker Quaid," he ground out. "Lucas is my twin. Not me."

A beat of silence. Then movement in his periphery.

Shannon, standing stiff, arms crossed, eyes locked on

him like she was trying to solve a puzzle she didn't expect to have in front of her. Her gaze flicked upward toward his scar. She noticed.

He held her stare, waiting for her to say anything, but she didn't. Her fingers curled slightly around her purse strap. Not as confident as she had been at the ranch.

Parker's chest tightened. She wasn't fully convinced anymore. But did it even matter? Not if the deputies didn't believe him. Not if Lucas had left enough wreckage behind to make Parker look guilty again.

———

THIS SHOULD HAVE felt like vindication. Like justice finally being served after eight years of carrying the scars Lucas Quaid left behind.

And yet the longer Shannon stood there, watching him, the more doubt twisted deep inside her. Because the way Lucas Quaid—Parker Quaid?—looked at her revealed nothing. No flicker of recognition. No tightening of his jaw like he knew exactly who she was, but was trying to play it cool.

Nothing.

Just sharp and simmering frustration, directed at the deputies, at the situation, but not at her. Like she was just another person in the room. Like he had never met her before in his life.

A chill crawled up her spine. That made no sense.

Lucas had sweet-talked her, woven himself into her life, made her believe they had real feelings for each other. Six months of shared laughter, whispered plans, stolen kisses. Six months of her thinking she might have finally found someone she could trust.

Yet, here he was, not even acknowledging her existence. Not angry. Not remorseful. Not mocking, smug, or defensive. Just blank frustration, like he was genuinely confused about why he was here at all. Like he actually didn't know who she was.

Her stomach dropped.

But he had Lucas's face, Lucas's height, build, presence. Except the scar. The voice. The way his shoulders held tension differently than Lucas ever had.

The pieces weren't fitting. Shannon swallowed, throat constricting, fingers clutching her purse strap. This wasn't right. But if he wasn't Lucas, if she had made a mistake, then what had she done?

The air in the sheriff's office felt too sharp, too sterile, pressing against Shannon's skin like the past was trying to smother her. She sat rigid in the chair, hands clenched in her lap, eyes locked on the deputy across the desk. He introduced himself as Deputy Matthew Long.

She could do this.

He flipped open a file, gaze steady. "Tell us everything you know about Lucas Quaid."

Shannon swallowed hard. Her fingers trembled against her purse strap for half a second before she steadied them, like the simple contact could anchor her against the rush of panic swelling inside her.

She had met him at Northern Arizona University eight years ago, back when her life had felt predictable, secure. Back when she'd still trusted easily.

"He was a student at NAU," she started, voice clipped. She had recounted the story so many times over the years it came out feeling rehearsed. "At least, he said he was."

Deputy Long barely reacted. He just waited, pen hovering over his notepad.

Shannon exhaled sharply, pressing forward. "We met through a mutual friend," she continued, gaze flicking toward the holding room. "He was charming. Thoughtful. Said the right things, knew how to make people feel special."

Her breath hitched. Lucas used to look at her in a way that made her believe she mattered. Her voice came out

17

thinner now.

"He talked about the future as if it were real. Like we were moving towards something lasting."

The deputy waited, watching her. Shannon continued, forcing herself to just say it.

"But it was all a lie." She exhaled slowly, as if she could shake off the ache still wrapped around those words. "He stole my college funds. Funneled them out of my account. Left me scrambling, humiliated, and fighting to pay for my last two years."

Her throat closed. She had to look away because the memories weren't distant anymore. They were alive, twisting inside her, choking her just like they had the day she learned the truth. She gripped her purse strap harder.

Deputy Long's expression grew more thoughtful, his tone gentle but serious. "You're sure it's him?" he asked.

That simple question slammed into her chest like a wrecking ball. She opened her mouth. Nothing came out.

Her gaze flicked toward the holding room, even though she couldn't see him. Parker Quaid? His scar. His voice. His expression of absolute frustration, but not recognition.

This wasn't Lucas's smooth deflection under pressure, his practiced charm when cornered. This was genuine confusion. Raw frustration. Doubt crept in, dismantling everything she thought she knew.

Before she could stop herself, before she could pull back the uncertainty unraveling inside her, the words slipped out. "Could Lucas really have an identical twin?"

Silence.

The deputy studied her with understanding rather than suspicion, like he'd caught the crack forming in her certainty. Like he was waiting for her to admit she wasn't sure anymore.

Shannon's stomach plummeted. Had she just made a huge mistake?

Deputy Long sat back, exhaling as he studied her with

understanding rather than suspicion, setting down his pen. "We're running his prints now. If he's Lucas, we'll know soon enough. Identical twins may share DNA, but their fingerprints are unique. There's no way to fake that."

The certainty in his tone should have been reassuring. Instead, it made her stomach twist tighter, pressing against her conscience as if the walls were about to crumble down. She thrust her hand into her hair, fingers curling briefly before they caught in the tangled strands.

"I..." She hesitated, voice edged with doubt she couldn't hide.

The deputy's gaze remained steady, his tone already gentle but growing even more understanding. "Listen, this was an easy mistake to make, especially given what you've been through."

Wasn't that what she had convinced herself? That she couldn't be wrong? That Lucas Quaid had finally been caught, and that she had been the one to put him in handcuffs?

Her throat constricted, heartbeat echoing in her ears. If Parker Quaid wasn't Lucas, if she had done this to an innocent man, then what had she just set in motion?

He leaned forward slightly, his tone compassionate. "You're not to blame here. You were protecting yourself based on what you knew. But when those results come back, we're going to have a clear answer."

Shannon managed a nod, unable to find her voice.

Thirty minutes stretched into an eternity. Shannon sat stiffly in the chair, eyes locked on the holding room door, trying and failing to push down the twisting sensation in her stomach. The deputy had stepped out to check the fingerprint results nearly ten minutes ago. The wait was suffocating.

The door swung open, and Deputy Long strode back in, a folder tucked under his arm, expression unreadable. Shannon's breath hitched.

He settled into his chair, flipping open the folder, scanning the document inside. Finally, he looked up.

"The man in question," the deputy said, voice steady, "is Parker Quaid."

The words hit like a slap to the face. Shannon sat frozen, her pulse hammering so loudly she barely registered the rest of his sentence.

"Not wanted for any crimes. No warrants. Clean record."

Parker Quaid. Not Lucas.

Her throat tightened, fingers digging into her palms. Everything inside her wanted to reject the truth, to push back against the sharp edges of reality cutting into her. Parker Quaid was innocent. She had gotten this wrong, and she had just sent an innocent man to jail.

The weight of the mistake settled deep. Thick, suffocating, impossible to shake. She had been so sure. Now? She wasn't sure of anything at all.

Shannon struggled to find her composure. She glanced up at the deputy. "I'm sorry," she said. "For wasting your time."

Deputy Long exhaled, his expression kind but honest. "You didn't waste our time," he said evenly. "You believed you were doing the right thing. Sometimes that's all we can do with the information we have."

She nodded, but it did little to ease the tightness in her neck.

He studied her for a beat longer, then leaned forward, just slightly, lowering his voice like he understood that this moment wasn't easy for her. "You okay to drive?" he asked.

The question caught her off guard. She blinked, glancing at her hands. Her grip was tighter than she realized, her fingers pressing hard into her palms, as if she needed an anchor to hold on to. The tension sat deep in her muscles, wrapped around her breath, and pressed into the back of her skull.

"I..." She hesitated. "Yeah. I think so."

Deputy Long held her gaze a second longer, as if deciding whether to press the issue. "If you need someone to take you home or if there's someone you want to call to pick you up, just say the word."

Shannon shook her head. "No," she said, voice steadier now, though the ache beneath it hadn't quite eased. "I can manage."

Deputy Long nodded, then closed the folder in front of him, letting out a quiet breath. "Take care, Miss Burke."

Shannon pushed to her feet, her pulse still off-kilter, her mind still reeling. She had walked in here certain she had won. Now she was walking out, questioning everything.

3

THE INTERVIEW ROOM smelled of burned coffee and old paperwork, an institutional staleness that clung to government buildings everywhere. Parker sat rigidly in the metal chair. The fluorescent light above him buzzed intermittently, casting harsh shadows across the scratched table surface. His wrists still ached where the cuffs had been, a phantom pressure that would probably linger for hours.

They were running his fingerprints. Again.

He'd been through this routine enough times to know the timeline. Twenty minutes for processing, maybe thirty if they were thorough. Then either freedom or a very long conversation about Lucas. Probably a call to his attorney. Maybe a night in a jail cell.

The uncertainty gnawed at him, but not in the way it used to. Two months at Vargas Ranch had given him what he'd never had before—a place worth fighting for. Dylan and Adan treated him like a man, not a walking reminder of someone else's crimes. Even Dalton, the ranch manager, had nodded approval when Parker fixed the broken gate latch without being asked.

If he lost that because of today, because Shannon Burke had him arrested...

Parker dragged a hand through his hair, pushing the thought away. No point borrowing trouble when he already had plenty.

The door opened, and the deputy stepped in, carrying a manila folder. Mid-forties, graying at the temples, with the weathered look of someone who'd spent years dealing with the worst humanity had to offer. But his expression wasn't the usual cop mask Parker expected.

"You're clear," Deputy Long said, settling into the chair across from him. "Parker Quaid. Clean record, no warrants."

The words should have brought instant relief. Instead, Parker's shoulders remain locked, the tension refusing to release after being wound so tight for so long.

"Thank you," he managed.

"This kind of thing must happen a lot."

Parker blinked, caught off guard. "More than you'd think."

Deputy Long nodded, making a note in the folder. "Well, for what it's worth, we'll be watching for false reports tied to your name. And if we do get called out again?" He tapped Parker's driver's license. "We'll start with this instead of assumptions."

In five arrests, countless interrogations, and years of suspicious stares, no one had ever acknowledged what it might actually be like to live in Lucas's shadow. Or reassured him that things would be different going forward.

"For what it's worth," the deputy gathered the folder and stood. "I can tell you're not the same person. Different way of carrying yourself, different way of talking. Different way of looking at people."

Parker's chest loosened, just slightly. "How so?"

"Your brother, based on what I've read in these files, looks at people like they're marks. Like he's calculating what he can get from them." The deputy tapped the folder. "You look at people like you're trying to figure out if they're going to hurt you first."

The observation hit harder than Parker expected. The silence thickened for a moment, the fluorescent light continuing its irregular buzz.

Then, Deputy Long extended his hand. "Take care of yourself, Parker."

Parker shook the offered hand, surprised by the firm grip and the genuine concern in the man's eyes. "Thank you. Really."

"Just doing my job."

The deputy moved toward the door and gestured down the corridor. "Exit's that way. You need a ride somewhere? I know you came in the cruiser."

The kind offer nearly undid him. "I'll figure something out."

"Alright. Take it easy."

Parker walked down the empty hallway, still wrestling with the strangest arrest experience of his life. A deputy who actually listened. Who saw him as separate from Lucas. Who offered help instead of suspicion.

He rolled his shoulders to ease the tension that had been building since this morning. His body felt heavy, drained from the adrenaline crash, but his mind was clearer than it had been in hours.

Time to figure out how to get home.

He stepped into the lobby, pulling his phone from his pocket to call for a ride. What he found instead was Shannon Burke.

She stood near the entrance, arms wrapped around herself as if she was trying to hold herself together. Her dark hair had flattened from whatever style she'd attempted this morning.

When she saw him, she straightened, but didn't approach.

Parker paused, studying her. The fire that had blazed in her eyes back at the stables was gone, replaced by what looked suspiciously like shame. Her fingers worried the strap of her purse, and she kept glancing at him then looking away.

For a moment, neither of them moved.

Then Shannon took a step forward, her voice barely above a whisper. "I'm sorry."

The words hung between them, simple and devastating. His walls cracked as a sliver of empathy for her broke through.

"I was so sure," she continued, her voice cracking slightly. "After what Lucas did to me, I thought... I never considered..."

She broke off, shaking her head.

He watched her struggle, recognizing what he'd felt countless times himself — the helpless frustration of trying to explain the unexplainable, of wanting to make it right after the damage was already done.

"You were protecting yourself," he said.

Shannon's eyes widened as they met his, her lips parting slightly like she hadn't expected understanding. "That doesn't make it right."

"No," Parker agreed. "But it makes it human."

"You don't have a way back to the ranch," she said.

"I'll call someone."

"I could..." Shannon worried her lower lip between her teeth. "I could drive you. If you're willing to let me try to make this right, even in some small way."

Parker hesitated. Every instinct told him to walk away, to avoid another person Lucas had hurt. But her shoulders rolled forward, and she took a step back, as if bracing for rejection.

She was another casualty of his brother's cons. Another person trying to rebuild from the destruction Lucas left behind.

Maybe they understood each other better than he realized.

"Alright," he said finally. "Let's go."

Shannon's features softened, and her shoulders relaxed. She nodded quickly, fishing car keys from her purse with hands that trembled just slightly.

"Thank you," she whispered.

Parker followed her toward the parking lot. The sun hung low near the horizon, and the air had turned surprisingly cool. He'd forgotten how fast the desert shed its daytime heat — warm when they'd walked into the sheriff's office, but now carrying the first hint of evening chill.

He still wasn't sure whether accepting her offer was smart or foolish. But right now, it beat walking. Even if the ride home was going to be the most awkward twenty minutes of his life.

————

THE SILENCE STRETCHED between them, thick and uncomfortable, as Shannon guided her car onto the highway. Parker sat rigid in the passenger seat, his gaze fixed on the desert landscape rolling past, shoulders tense as if bracing for the next blow.

She had done this to him.

The thought sat heavy in her chest, pressing against her ribs with each breath. She'd seen his face and immediately jumped to conclusions, called the sheriff, watched him get handcuffed and dragged away like a common criminal. All because she couldn't separate the man beside her from the one who'd destroyed her life eight years ago.

But even now, sitting in the charged quiet of her car, she could feel the differences. Parker's silence wasn't sharp or calculating. It was wounded. Where Lucas had filled every pause with charm or deflection, Parker existed in the space between words, solid and present despite his obvious pain.

"I owe you an explanation," she whispered, breaking the silence.

Parker's jaw tightened, but he didn't respond. Didn't even look at her. His hands remained still on his knees, steady where Lucas's would have been restless, drumming with nervous energy or gesturing for effect.

Shannon swallowed hard. "What Lucas did to me—it wasn't just about money. He took everything I had saved for college. Even the small emergency fund my great-aunt had helped me build."

She sensed the weight of his attention settle on her, quiet and unmoving. Even his listening felt different. Patient rather than predatory, like he was absorbing her words instead of calculating how to use them.

"I was a sophomore at NAU when it happened. One day I had enough to finish my degree. The next day my accounts were empty, and Lucas was gone." The words came out steadier than she'd expected, probably because she'd recounted them so many times. "I had to fight just to stay in school. Prove I wasn't reckless or irresponsible, and that someone had actually stolen from me."

Parker shifted slightly, releasing his grip on his knee. The slight movement drew her attention to his hands. Calloused from honest work, scarred from ranch life. His hands showed evidence of genuine labor, not the smooth palms Lucas had maintained through a lifetime of avoiding responsibility.

"The worst part wasn't even the financial mess," Shannon continued, her voice growing stronger as she recognized the safety in Parker's stillness. "I thought I loved him. Thought he loved me. I was planning a future with someone who intended to rob me. I never saw it coming."

She exhaled shakily.

"So when I saw your face today, all of that came rushing back. The betrayal, the humiliation, the anger I've been carrying. I reacted instead of thinking."

When she glanced at Parker's profile, the late afternoon light caught the scar above his eyebrow. The small imperfection somehow made him more real than Lucas's practiced perfection had ever been.

"You mentioned that scar earlier," Shannon said, the

question forming before she could second-guess it. "Where'd you get it?"

Parker's hand lifted briefly toward his left eyebrow before dropping back to his knee. "Ranch accident when I was six. Playing too close to some equipment, and hit my head on the edge." His tone was matter-of-fact, with no drama or embellishment. "Bled like crazy. Scared my mom half to death."

The straightforward honesty of it struck her. No performance, no story crafted for sympathy. Just a simple answer. The real, unvarnished truth. Lucas would never have stated it so concisely. He would have made himself look heroic or victimized, never just... human.

Silence settled for a few beats before Parker spoke again, his voice rough but steady. "How long did you know him?"

The question held no judgment, no manipulation. Just genuine curiosity. Shannon's shoulders loosened slightly at the honest concern in his tone.

"Six months. Long enough to think I understood who he was. Long enough to let him convince me to trust him with access to my accounts for some fake emergency. Long enough to feel like the biggest fool on the planet when I realized what he'd done."

Parker was quiet for a moment. When he spoke again, his tone had lost some of its edge, replaced by something that sounded like understanding.

"That's what he does. Finds people's vulnerabilities and uses them."

The matter-of-fact way he said it struck her. No bitterness, no anger, just weary acceptance. She couldn't imagine how many times he must have been forced to clean up after his brother's messes.

"Is that what happened to you too?" The question slipped out before Shannon could stop it. "I mean, obviously not the same way, but—"

"He cost me jobs. Relationships. Got me arrested more

times than I can count." Parker's voice was calm, but Shannon heard the weariness underneath. And something else. Dignity. Quiet strength that had somehow survived years of bearing blame for crimes he'd never committed. "People see this face and assume they know what kind of man I am. Usually they're wrong, but that doesn't stop them from judging me."

Shame washed over her like a physical blow. She'd done the same thing. Seen his face and decided who he was without giving him a chance to prove otherwise. But even as guilt twisted in her stomach, she marveled at his composure. Lucas would have made himself the victim, would have used her mistake to gain sympathy or an advantage. Parker simply acknowledged the reality without self-pity.

"How do you stand it?" she asked quietly, genuinely wanting to understand how someone could endure so much injustice without becoming bitter. "Being judged for someone else's choices?"

Parker huffed a short laugh, devoid of humor but somehow not cruel. "You learn to expect it. Hope for better, but expect the worst."

The resignation in his voice made her shoulders tense. She stole a glance at his profile, noting the way he held himself. Not defeated, but carefully guarded. Protecting himself without closing off entirely. It was a delicate balance she recognized from her own journey of learning to trust again.

They drove in silence for a few minutes, the lights of Vargas Ranch growing closer.

"I'm supposed to meet with Dylan and Adan tomorrow morning," she said as they turned onto the ranch's access road. "About the equine therapy charity position. If I cost you your job because of my mistake—"

"I don't know. It might," Parker said, his fingers tightening against his knee. "Has before. At other places."

The honesty in his voice was harder to hear than false confidence would have been, causing Shannon's stomach to clench. She wanted to reassure him, to promise everything would be fine, but something about Parker's straightforward acceptance of reality made empty platitudes feel insulting.

"What do you mean?"

Parker was quiet as she pulled up to the stables, the engine ticking in the sudden silence. He reached for the door handle but didn't immediately get out, and Shannon held her breath, afraid he'd leave without explaining, afraid she'd lose this fragile connection before she fully understood it.

"I mean, I've only been here two months," he said finally, his voice barely above a whisper but carrying more weight than any shout. "Dylan and Adan seem like good men, but I've thought that about employers before. Most of them decide it's easier to let me go than to deal with whatever drama Lucas's history brings."

"They're different," Shannon said, though the words felt hollow even as she spoke them. How could she know? She'd met them once. Today. In the middle of her hysterics. Heat warmed her face as she realized how inadequate her reassurance sounded.

Parker's smile was grim but not unkind. "Maybe. I hope so. But hope doesn't always change reality."

Shannon held back a sigh. She'd put his fragile sense of security at risk with her rash actions and had potentially destroyed his latest fresh start when he'd already lost too much.

"It's the first time in years I've felt like I might actually belong somewhere," Parker admitted, his voice barely above a whisper. The honesty of it hit her like a physical blow, and she leaned slightly toward him, drawn by the genuine vulnerability he was offering. "If that's gone now..."

He didn't finish the sentence, but Shannon heard what he wasn't saying. If he lost this job, this place that had begun to feel like home, because of her mistake, he'd be back to starting over in places where nobody knew his name or his brother's reputation. The thought made her stomach twist.

"Parker," she said as he started to climb out of the car, her hand moving instinctively toward his arm before she caught herself. "I know you have no reason to trust me, but if there's anything I can do to make this right — anything at all — please let me know."

He paused, half in and half out of the car, studying her face in the soft glow from the barn's security lights. For a moment, Shannon thought he might brush off her offer. But as his blue eyes met hers — so much clearer and steadier than Lucas's had ever been — she saw something shift in his expression.

"I'll keep that in mind."

It wasn't forgiveness. It wasn't even friendship. Only a willingness to consider that maybe she wasn't just another person who'd decided who he was based on his brother's reputation. And as that small opening appeared, Shannon felt something dangerous stirring in her heart. Not just the desire to make amends, but genuine curiosity about the man beneath the familiar face.

"Good luck tomorrow with Dylan and Adan," he said, closing the car door with a quiet click.

Shannon watched him walk to his truck, noting the weariness in the set of his shoulders. She noticed the way he moved with purpose and quiet grace, nothing like Lucas's performative swagger. As his headlights disappeared down the road toward what she assumed was employee housing, she started her car and drove home, her mind churning with thoughts she wasn't ready to examine.

4

PARKER WALKED TO his truck on unsteady legs, gravel crunching beneath his boots. The familiar weight of his keys felt foreign, like his hands had forgotten how to work.

Instinctively, his fingers twitched toward his wrists, rubbing slowly, absently, as if the cuffs still lingered cold against his skin, even though they were long gone. He should be used to it by now, but he wasn't.

He climbed into the cab and sat for a moment, dropping his head back against the seat, breathing in the scent of car freshener and the faint trace of horses clinging to his clothes. His mind was a storm he couldn't quiet.

Shannon Burke had looked at him like she was still trying to figure him out, still wrestling with the resemblance she couldn't shake. And honestly? He got it. Even now, after proving he wasn't Lucas, his twin's deception had felt like a stain he'd never scrub clean. In her view. Maybe in Dylan's and Adan's too.

He exhaled sharply, turned the key, and the truck rumbled to life. The drive to the dining hall was short, the ranch quiet and dark save for the lights casting long shadows along the road.

By the time he pulled into the lot, most of the tables inside were empty. The scent of warm food lingered in the air as the kitchen crew started cleaning up after the dinner service. Parker stepped inside, scanning the buffet line. Mostly picked over, with a few trays still sitting out. He grabbed a to-go container, filling it with just enough to refuel, even though the knot in his stomach almost made eating feel pointless. Hungry but not. Needing the energy. That was all.

He settled at a corner table, back to the wall, gaze flicking toward the exit, trying to focus on the rote motions. The food was good—roast beef, mashed potatoes, green beans that actually had flavor. He forced himself to take slow bites, letting the familiar routine of a meal ground him after the chaos of the afternoon.

Then his gaze drifted to the stenciled words painted on the far wall, the familiar verses catching in his mind before he could pull away. *With regard to the works of man, by the word of your lips I have avoided the ways of the violent. My steps have held fast to your paths; my feet have not slipped.* Psalm 17:4–5. The Vargas family verses. Not his, but the ones he'd seen every day since stepping onto the ranch two months ago. They were in the dining hall, in the barn office, even stitched onto Dalton's saddle blanket like a quiet declaration of what this place stood for.

Parker exhaled slowly, rubbing a hand along his jaw. Held fast. Hadn't slipped. He wasn't sure if that was true for him, no matter how hard he had tried to pull himself out of Lucas's shadow. The Vargas men believed in those words, but Parker had spent his whole life wondering if the world had already decided who he was, long before he ever got a say.

He finished eating and stepped outside, the cool evening air wrapping around him, crisp with the lingering scent of dust and the faint trace of horses drifting from the stables. The truck cab felt smaller now, confining, as he started the engine and pulled out of the lot toward the bunkhouse.

The short drive gave his mind too much room to wander. Today could have been the last straw. Dylan's jaw had gone tight. Adan had said nothing in his defense. The sheriff's deputies showing up at the ranch, cuffing him in front of employees. Maybe that had crossed a line he couldn't uncross. Maybe he was more trouble than he was worth.

Parker turned the last corner toward the bunkhouse, and his stomach dropped.

Dylan and Adan stood on the porch, silhouetted against the warm light spilling from the windows. Waiting.

He pulled into his usual parking spot, hands gripping the steering wheel as he scanned the porch area. No cardboard boxes. No trash bags stuffed with his belongings. No clear sign that he'd been fired while sitting in the station.

That had to be a good sign. Right?

Parker cut the engine and climbed out of the truck. Dylan and Adan hadn't moved, their gazes tracking his approach across the gravel lot. The crunch of his footsteps seemed unnaturally loud in the evening's stillness.

He'd been through this before. The careful conversation where employers explained that his situation made him a liability. The apologetic tone that couldn't quite hide their relief at having an excuse to let him go. The boxes of his things waiting by the door like evidence of how easily he could be erased.

But there were no boxes tonight.

Dylan nodded once as Parker approached the porch steps. "You got a minute?"

Parker swallowed hard. He could make an excuse, delay whatever conversation was coming. But that would only make it worse.

"Yeah," he said, climbing the steps toward whatever verdict they'd reached.

Parker stepped onto the porch, the wood creaking softly beneath his boots, the light spilling across the worn planks in patches of gold. The silence stretched between the three men, heavy with unspoken questions. Dylan leaned against the post, arms crossed, while Adan rested his forearms against the porch railing, both of them studying Parker with expressions he couldn't quite read.

The lack of boxes on the porch had given him a sliver of hope. But now, facing their serious faces in the dim light, that hope felt fragile.

It was Adan who finally broke the silence. "We want to hear what happened today. Your side of it."

Parker's shoulders tensed. Not immediate judgment. They wanted facts first. He could respect that.

"Shannon Burke thought I was my twin brother," Parker said, keeping his voice steady. "Lucas. He's the one with the criminal record. She called the sheriff before I could convince her otherwise."

Dylan nodded slowly. "Go on."

"I tried to explain. Showed her my scar, told her I wasn't him. But she was convinced I was lying." Parker rubbed the back of his neck. "Lucas stole her college money eight years ago."

"That why she was so certain?" Adan asked.

"Wouldn't you be?" Parker met his gaze. "If someone destroyed your life, and you thought you'd found them again, you'd want justice too."

Adan nodded with a glimmer of understanding.

"Fingerprints cleared it up," Parker continued. "Sheriff confirmed I'm not Lucas. Shannon apologized. Gave me a ride back."

The facts sounded simple when he laid them out like that. Clean, straightforward. But they didn't capture the weight of being handcuffed again, the familiar humiliation of proving his identity, the exhaustion of this recurring nightmare.

Dylan was quiet for a long moment, his gaze steady on Parker's face. When he spoke, his voice was measured. "You didn't do anything wrong."

Parker blinked, unsure if he heard him right.

Adan straightened. "We don't punish men for mistakes their brother made. We don't assume guilt just because someone else shares your appearance."

"But?" Parker asked.

"No but," Dylan said. "You're not your brother. We knew that when we hired you, and we know it now."

Parker's chest loosened. "Even after today?"

"Especially after today," Adan said. "You handled yourself well. Stayed calm, cooperated with law enforcement. That tells us who you are better than any background check could."

The words settled into Parker's bones. They weren't firing him. Or treating him as if his brother's crimes were contagious. He scarcely believed it.

"Dalton feels the same way," Dylan added. "We briefed him. His words were, 'twins aren't responsible for each other's choices.'"

Parker's throat tightened. "I don't know what to say."

"Don't say anything," Adan replied. "Just show up tomorrow ready to work."

Dylan pushed away from the post. "Get some rest."

Adan lingered a moment longer, reaching out to squeeze Parker's shoulder. "We'll see you in the morning."

The door shut behind them, leaving Parker alone as the stars dotted the night sky, mirroring the thin thread of hope in his soul. The tension didn't fully ease as reality wrapped around him. He wasn't just an employee they were tolerating. He was someone they respected. And they wanted him to stay.

For the first time in longer than he could remember, Parker believed he might actually belong somewhere. Not because he'd hidden from his past, but because he'd found people who saw him for the man he really was.

———

THE DESERT STRETCHED wide in front of Shannon as the early morning light cast long slants of gold across the highway. Unfortunately, the serene landscape did nothing to quiet her thoughts.

She had believed Lucas once so deeply that she'd ignored the signs, dismissed the unease, and convinced herself she saw the real him. And she'd been wrong. Then yesterday, she'd trusted her own instincts again, certain Parker was Lucas, sure she wasn't making another mistake. Wrong again.

She inhaled sharply, exhaling through her mouth. If she had misjudged both brothers so completely, what did that say about her instincts? The worst part was that Lucas had fooled her on purpose. But Parker? He had done nothing to mislead her.

The weight settled low in her stomach, a dull ache she couldn't shake. How many other assumptions had she made in her life? How many times had she been completely certain, only to be completely wrong?

Shannon stepped out of her car, smoothing her hands down the front of her shirt, willing her nerves to settle. Focus on the meeting. That was what mattered.

She took a steadying breath, heading toward the stable office, but stopped short when she spotted Parker stepping out of the barn, wiping his hands against a rag.

He saw her but didn't stop walking.

Shannon bit her lower lip. She could let him pass. She could avoid making this worse.

Instead, she spoke. "Parker."

He slowed, his posture stiff but not dismissive.

She forced herself to meet his gaze. "I just need to say I'm sorry. Again. I was so sure. And I was so wrong."

The low hum of morning activity filled the space where words should have been.

Parker didn't answer right away, just studied her, unreadable and quiet. Finally, he gave a slow nod. Not forgiveness, but acknowledgement.

She clasped her hands in front of her, twisting her fingers. "I have to meet with Dylan and Adan." She motioned toward the stables, eager for an exit.

When she turned to leave, Parker spoke. "Good luck."

"Thanks."

Then she headed toward the office. The weight of their interaction lingered longer than she expected.

Nearing the office, Shannon squared her shoulders and rapped her knuckles against the open door frame. The scent of leather and dust filled the space.

"Morning. C-c-come in." Dylan gestured from where he leaned against the filing cabinet.

Adan set aside some papers, studying her with quiet intensity. "Have a seat."

She settled across from him, angling her chair to see both men.

"Before we get into details," Adan said, "you should know why this matters to us. Braden's my nephew, my sister Brisa's boy. He's a double amputee and uses prosthetics. When he first saw horses here, he wanted to ride more than anything. Wouldn't take no for an answer."

Dylan's expression grew tender. "Standard saddles wouldn't work. So, I researched adaptive equipment. Found a specialized saddle designed for double amputees."

"Cost more than most people's monthly salary," Adan added. "But watching Braden discover he could be a cowboy just like any other kid — that he could do something nobody thought was possible — it changed everything."

Dylan's voice was quiet but steady. "Kids like Braden shouldn't have to wonder if they b-b-belong somewhere."

"So we pooled our resources," Adan said. "Hired an equine therapy instructor. If we could help one kid feel that confidence, imagine what we could do for dozens. Veterans too."

Shannon sat quietly for a moment, absorbing what they'd shared. This wasn't just a business opportunity. This was an invitation to something life-changing.

"That's what I want to be part of," she said. "Building something that gives kids and veterans that kind of hope."

Adan studied her, then nodded. "Still want the job?"

She smiled and replied quickly. "Yes."

"Alright," Adan said. "So what's your vision for launching this properly?"

Shannon straightened. "A fundraising gala. Early December. Gives us just enough time to pull it together while capitalizing on year-end giving. I have connections throughout Phoenix's philanthropic community who respond well to elegant events with a compelling mission."

"That's ambitious," Dylan said. "Six weeks to plan a gala?"

"I've done it before," Shannon said. "And Braden's Hope deserves a strong launch."

"Tell us what you need," Adan said.

Shannon explained her vision in more detail. A fancy evening catering to Phoenix's philanthropic community, complete with an auction of high-end items and experiences. When she finished, both Adan and Dylan were on board.

Adan leaned back in his chair. "Alright. Make it happen."

Dylan pushed away from the filing cabinet. "You're going to need help. Parker knows where we keep event supplies—tables, chairs, what needs renting versus what's available. He can show you around."

Shannon's nerves flared, but she held steady. She'd earned the discomfort.

"I'll grab him," Dylan said.

A few minutes later, Parker appeared in the doorway, his gaze finding Shannon before flicking to Adan. His jaw tightened almost imperceptibly.

"You needed me?"

Dylan nodded. "Shannon's organizing a charity gala for Braden's Hope in early December. You'll help her figure out what equipment we have versus what needs renting."

Parker's eyes flicked to Shannon again. A beat of silence stretched.

"Sure," he said finally. "Whatever you need."

But Shannon caught the slight tension in his voice, the way his hands curled into loose fists before he relaxed them.

"Great. Shannon, Parker can show you around this afternoon."

"That would be perfect," Shannon said, though her voice sounded strained.

Parker's gaze shifted toward the door. "Just let me know when."

"Two o'clock?"

"Fine. I'll meet you at the dining hall."

And then he was gone, leaving Shannon staring at the empty doorway, wondering how she was going to navigate working with a man she'd wrongfully had arrested less than twenty-four hours ago.

But that wasn't the only thing unsettling her. Despite sharing Lucas's appearance, there was something about Parker that drew her in ways Lucas never had. Maybe it was the quiet strength in the way he carried himself, or the restraint he'd shown when he had every right to be angry.

"Thank you," she said to Adan and Dylan. "For trusting me with this. I won't let you down."

Adan's smile was warm. "We're counting on it."

5

PARKER COILED THE lead rope around his hand as he approached the arena, the braided fibers smoothed by years of use. The November afternoon had settled into that perfect desert temperature—warm with a breeze that carried the scent of palo verde trees and the distant sound of cattle lowing in the pasture.

Braden's session with Lorissa was just beginning, and Parker had timed his arrival to watch. The kid's laughter rang out clear and joyful, a sound that could soften even the most cynical ranch hand. Parker had learned to treasure these moments. Not just because they represented hope for kids like Braden, but because they reminded him why the work mattered.

He reached the arena fence just as Lorissa guided Miracle toward the special mounting platform they'd installed. It had stairs on one side and a lift on the other. The bay mare's ears pricked forward with the alertness that came from a horse who genuinely enjoyed her job. Braden sat tall in the saddle, his small hands gripping the reins with confidence that had grown week by week since Parker had started working at Vargas Ranch.

"Look at me, Parker!" Braden called out, spotting him immediately. "Lorissa says I can try steering by myself today!"

"Show me what you've got, buddy," Parker replied, settling his forearms on the top rail of the fence.

He spotted Shannon twenty feet away, her fingers wrapped around the metal fencing, her attention completely absorbed by the scene unfolding in the arena. She stood motionless, watching Braden with an expression Parker hadn't seen before — unguarded and full of wonder.

When Braden successfully guided Miracle through a gentle turn, Shannon placed a hand over her heart.

"Excellent work, Braden," Lorissa called, bringing Miracle to a halt near the center of the arena. "You're really getting the hang of riding."

Braden beamed, his whole body radiating pride. "Did you see, Miss Shannon? I did it all by myself!"

Shannon startled slightly, as if she'd forgotten anyone else existed beyond the miracle she was witnessing. She moved closer to the fence, her voice soft when she spoke.

"I saw everything, Braden. You looked amazing up there."

"Parker helps get the horses ready for us," Braden announced with the matter-of-fact tone of a four-year-old sharing important information. "He makes sure they're not scared and that they know what to do. And then after, he takes care of them so they're not tired."

Heat crept up Parker's neck.

When Shannon turned to look at him, her eyes widened. Her head cocked to the side as if expecting to see someone else.

"That's very thoughtful," she said, her gaze holding his for a moment before returning to Braden. "The horses are lucky to have someone who cares about them."

"Parker cares about everyone," Braden declared with absolute certainty. "Even when people are mean to him, he's still nice. That's what Mom says makes him special."

The words hit Parker like a physical blow. This kid saw kindness as a strength rather than a weakness, saw caring as something that made a person special rather than vulnerable. What an incredible gift. Hopefully, Braden wouldn't grow out of that quality.

Shannon's breath caught, and when she looked at Parker again, her eyes softened. The wariness from yesterday was gone, replaced by the beginning of something else. Understanding, maybe. Or trust.

"All right, my friend," Lorissa called to Braden, "let's get you down from there so Miracle can have her well-deserved break."

Parker pushed away from the fence, fishing the halter from his back pocket as he crossed into the ring. The familiar routine grounded him as he checked Miracle's girth, running his hands along her legs to ensure no heat or swelling, speaking to her in the low, calm tones that helped horses transition from work to rest.

"She did good today," he told Braden as the boy carefully descended from the mounting platform, his prosthetics clicking softly against the metal steps.

"She's the best horse ever," Braden replied with the fierce loyalty of a child who'd found his favorite. "Will you tell her I said thank you?"

Parker's throat tightened unexpectedly. "I'll make sure she knows."

As Braden headed toward the arena exit where his mother waited, Parker clipped the lead rope to Miracle's halter and began the cooldown routine. A few easy laps around the arena to let her muscles relax.

When Shannon fell into step beside them, her heeled boots tapped out a different rhythm against the arena's footing than the hollow thud of his worn work boots.

"How long has he been in the program?" she asked.

"About two months. Started right after I did." Parker glanced at her sideways. "He was pretty hesitant at first. Took three sessions before he'd even touch Miracle, let alone get in the saddle."

"And now?"

"Now he talks about wanting to be a cowboy when he grows up." Parker couldn't keep the pride out of his voice. "Says he's going to have his own ranch and help other kids learn to ride."

Shannon was quiet for several steps. When Parker looked at her again, he saw tears threatening to spill over her lower lashes.

"This is why you wanted the job," he said. "Not just the charity work, but this. Seeing kids like Braden discover what they're capable of."

"Kids like Braden, veterans struggling with the scars of war, and anyone who needs to remember their own strength." Shannon's voice carried a passion that transformed her entire demeanor. "Horses don't see limitations. They respond to intention, to the heart. They give people back pieces of themselves they thought were lost forever."

The conviction in her words struck something deep in Parker's chest. This wasn't someone playing at charity work to fill time or build a resume. She meant every word.

Shannon reached out to stroke Miracle's neck, and the mare lowered her head immediately.

"After college, after everything that happened, I threw myself into Aunt Shirley's charity. It was good work, important work, but safe work. Predictable outcomes, measurable progress." Shannon kept her hand on Miracle's neck. "But when my aunt told me about what the Vargas family was building here, something clicked. This isn't just therapy. It's transformational. It's watching someone like Braden discover he's not defined by what he's lost, but by what he chooses to do with what he has."

They'd reached the barn entrance, and Parker led Miracle inside. The temperature dropped a few degrees in the shade, and the familiar scents of hay and leather surrounded them.

As Parker moved Miracle into the cross-ties, his mind

circled back to what he'd just witnessed. Shannon hadn't watched Braden just with sympathy or professional interest. She'd understood something fundamental about what had happened in that arena. The way she'd moved around Miracle during the cooldown, the natural ease in her posture, the confidence when she'd touched the mare weren't things someone could fake.

She'd grown up around horses. Had to have.

But more than that, she'd taken whatever hurt Lucas had caused and turned it into something that helped others heal. That took courage. And purpose.

He picked up the body brush, working it over Miracle's coat in long, steady strokes. Shannon leaned against the barn wall, watching him work. The afternoon light filtering through the windows caught the brown of her hair, turning it warm gold at the edges.

"Sounds like you found your calling," he said.

"I hope so. And I hope I can make the gala something that honors Braden's Hope."

Parker moved the brush across Miracle's shoulder, processing everything he'd learned about Shannon today. She wasn't just Lucas's ex-girlfriend anymore. She wasn't just another person caught in his twin's wake of destruction.

She was someone who understood this work. Who cared about the same things he cared about. Who belonged here in a way he hadn't expected.

The realization settled over him like the warm desert sun.

"You grew up around horses," he said.

"Some. Aunt Shirley had a small place when I was younger. Nothing like this, but I learned the basics." Shannon's smile was soft, touched with nostalgia. "I'd forgotten how much I missed it until today."

"It shows." The words came out rougher than he'd intended. "The way you move around them, how you read their body language. That's not something you can fake."

She looked surprised by the observation, color rising in her cheeks. "I wasn't sure if I'd embarrass myself."

"Not even close." Parker moved to Miracle's other side, hyperaware of Shannon's presence just a few feet away. "You belong here."

The words hung between them, carrying more weight than he'd meant them to. But he couldn't deny the truth of it. Shannon fit at Vargas Ranch. The certainty of that shot through him quiet and sure.

"Thank you," she whispered, and something in her tone made him look up from Miracle's shoulder.

Their eyes met across the mare's back, and Parker felt the air shift between them. Not the careful politeness of yesterday or the professional collaboration of this morning, but something deeper. Recognition, maybe. Or possibility.

The moment stretched longer than it should have; neither of them looked away. Parker's hands stilled on the brush, his pulse picking up as he studied Shannon's face in the golden barn light. The gentle curve of her mouth, the way her dark eyes reflected the warm glow from the windows, the trust he could see building there despite everything they'd been through.

This was dangerous territory. Shannon was Lucas's ex-girlfriend. He shouldn't be noticing the strand of hair that had escaped from behind her ear or wondering what it would feel like to smooth it back himself.

But watching her today—seeing her genuine care for the kids, her natural ease with the horses, the passion in her voice when she talked about the work—he couldn't pretend he didn't feel the pull toward her.

Miracle shifted restlessly, breaking the spell. Parker cleared his throat and went back to brushing, but the awareness remained. Shannon was no longer just Lucas's victim or even just a colleague. She was becoming something else entirely. Something that made his chest tight and his hands unsteady.

Something dangerous and wonderful at the same time.

"Come on," he said, unclipping Miracle from the cross-ties and leading her toward her stall. His voice sounded steadier than he felt. "Let me show you around the rest of the facilities. If you're going to pull off this gala, you need to see everything we have to work with."

"I'd like that," she said, twisting a strand of hair around her finger.

As they headed deeper into the barn, Parker wondered if maybe Dylan had understood something he hadn't when he'd paired them together. Maybe Shannon wasn't just someone who needed help with logistics. Maybe she was someone who could see him for who he really was. As Parker. Not Lucas.

———

SHANNON WALKED BESIDE Parker toward the dining hall, processing the change that had occurred between them at the arena. Watching him with Braden had altered everything. Not just her perception of him, but her willingness to let down the walls she'd built around her heart. The afternoon sun cast long shadows across the pathways, and she stole glances at Parker as he pointed out various ranch buildings, his voice carrying quiet confidence.

"The dining hall doubles as our event space," he said, pulling open one of the glass doors. "Drake handles the restaurant side. He'll want to coordinate with you on the catering."

Shannon entered and stopped short, her breath catching at the sheer scope of the space. Massive log beams stretched overhead like the ribs of some great cathedral, while floor-to-ceiling glass panels along the far wall promised seamless indoor-outdoor flow. The late afternoon light poured through those windows, illuminating distressed walls decorated with turquoise pottery and wrought iron crosses.

"This is absolutely perfect," she breathed, her mind immediately shifting into planning mode. She walked toward the center of the room, arms spreading as she envisioned the transformation. "We could open those glass panels and set up portable heaters for comfort. String café lights across the patio. The fireplace area would work beautifully as an intimate conversation space."

She turned in a slow circle, her excitement building with each detail she noticed. "And if we position the main presentation area here, Dylan and Adan would be silhouetted against the outdoor lighting. It would be magical."

"You're seeing the entire event, aren't you?" Parker's observation carried a note of admiration that sent warmth through her.

"I can't help it," Shannon admitted, feeling heat rise in her cheeks. "When I see a space like this, my brain starts redesigning it automatically. The log beams are perfect for hanging decorations that will complement rather than compete with Christmas décor. When do you typically decorate for the holidays?"

"Day after Thanksgiving, it's all hands on deck. Even the ranch hands get drafted for garland duty." The hint of amusement in Parker's voice made her look at him more closely, noting the way his mouth almost curved into a smile.

Shannon nodded, already calculating timelines. Early December for the gala meant working with full holiday decorations, which could either be a blessing or a nightmare depending on execution.

"Hey there! You must be Shannon."

She turned to see a young man emerging from what appeared to be a coffee shop area tucked into one corner of the dining hall. With his dark hair pulled into a neat man bun and an aesthetic that somehow perfectly blended hipster and cowboy—vintage band t-shirt, fitted jeans, well-worn boots—he looked like he could belong in Portland as much as Arizona.

"I'm Drake Vargas," he said, extending his hand with a genuine warmth that made Shannon immediately like him. "Parker mentioned you're planning a charity gala. That's incredible."

"Shannon Burke," she replied, shaking his hand and matching his enthusiasm. "This space has so much potential. I was just telling Parker how perfectly it could work for what we're envisioning."

"Oh man, you should see it during the Christmas season," Drake said, his eyes lighting up with the fervor of someone describing their favorite movie. "We put up this massive twenty-foot tree right there in that corner." He gestured toward the fireplace area. "Garland on every beam, lights everywhere. It's like walking into a Christmas movie."

Shannon's mind immediately began working around the tree placement, seeing how the natural focal point could anchor the entire event design. "That could actually be perfect. We could arrange the seating to flow around the tree. Use it as a backdrop for photos."

"And hey," Drake continued, practically bouncing with excitement, "I'd love to help with the food. I've got some ideas for a dessert station here at the coffee bar. Maybe something special for the charity?"

"That would be wonderful," Shannon said, feeling her own excitement building in response to his enthusiasm. Everything was falling into place better than she'd dared hope. "We'll definitely need to coordinate on the menu."

"Absolutely. Just let me know what you need." Drake glanced between Shannon and Parker. "Parker's been amazing to work with, by the way. He's learned more about our operations in two months than some people pick up in years."

Shannon caught the way Parker's back straightened slightly at the praise. She was recognizing the signs of a man unaccustomed to positive attention, someone who'd learned to brace for the other shoe to drop.

"We should check out the storage areas," Parker said, his tone carefully neutral. "See what kind of equipment and furnishings we have on hand."

"Good thinking," Shannon agreed. "Drake, thank you for offering to help. I'll be in touch once I have a better sense of the overall plan."

"Looking forward to it," Drake said with another warm smile before returning to his coffee station.

Parker led her toward a door near the kitchen area, and Shannon was acutely aware when his hand briefly touched her lower back to guide her around a table. The contact was polite, professional, but it sent an unexpected jolt through her system, one she consciously ignored.

The storage area was larger than she'd expected, filled with round tables, rectangular banquet tables, and stacks of chairs in various styles. Parker moved through the space with easy familiarity, explaining the capacity of different table sizes and pointing out the various options available.

"Linens are in here," he said, opening a large cabinet to reveal neatly folded black tablecloths. "Nothing fancy, but they're clean and professional."

Shannon watched his hands as he showed how the tables folded, noting the careful way he handled even basic equipment despite his obvious strength. Every movement was precise, deliberate. His actions conveyed his pride in doing things properly.

"This covers most of what we'll need," she said, running her fingers along the edge of one table. "We might need to rent a few specialty pieces, but this gives us an excellent foundation."

They stood in the storage room surrounded by the practical materials that would help transform her vision into reality. The space felt smaller with both of them in it, and Shannon became acutely aware of Parker's presence beside her. The steady rhythm of his breathing. The faint scent of leather and horses clung to his clothes.

"You really care about this," Parker said quietly, his voice carrying a weight that made her look up at him.

"I do," she admitted, tucking her hair behind her ear. "But so do you. I can see it in how you talk about Braden, in how you handle every detail here. This place is important to you."

He was quiet for a long moment, his gaze fixed on the stack of chairs beside them.

"I've worked at a lot of places," he said. "Most of them, you're just another set of hands. Clock in, do the work, clock out. But here..." He paused, seeming to weigh his words carefully. "Here, what you do actually matters. Not just the daily operations, but things like Braden's sessions. Watching that kid grow stronger every week, seeing him discover what he's capable of... it reminds you why some work is worth doing."

The conviction in his voice made her pulse quicken. His honesty drew her in, revealing depths she hadn't expected to find.

"I'm sorry," she said. "For yesterday, obviously, but also for all the assumptions I made before I really knew you."

When Parker looked at her, his expression softening, Shannon felt something shift between them. He was close enough that she could see the flecks of darker blue in his eyes, close enough that his quiet strength seemed to wrap around her like warmth.

"You're seeing me now," he whispered.

The words settled into her heart, gentle but profound. For a moment suspended in time, they looked at each other with new understanding. Her carefully maintained walls trembled, threatening to crumble under the weight of his steady kindness.

Then the sound of voices from the dining hall reminded her where they were, what they were supposed to be doing.

"We should—" she started, then cleared her throat.

"Look at that outdoor staging area tomorrow," Parker said, rubbing a hand on the back of his neck. "It's got pea gravel and good drainage. I think we've rented event tents for it before."

"That sounds perfect," Shannon managed, grateful he was giving her an escape route.

They headed back toward the main dining room, the practical conversation about logistics providing safe ground. But Shannon couldn't ignore the awareness humming between them now — the way Parker held the door for her, the careful space he maintained, the quiet competence that drew her in despite every instinct telling her to be careful.

As they reached the entrance, Parker paused. "For what it's worth," he said, "I think you're going to create something special for these kids. Braden's fortunate to have someone fighting for him who understands what healing looks like."

The sincerity in his voice, the way he looked at her like he genuinely believed in her vision, made Shannon's throat tight.

"Thank you," she whispered. "That means everything."

Standing there in the golden afternoon light filtering through the dining hall windows, Shannon's stomach coiled. She was walking into uncharted territory. Not because Parker resembled the man who'd betrayed her, but because he was proving to be everything Lucas had never been — genuine, thoughtful, and worthy of trust.

The possibility of caring for him terrified her more than any physical resemblance ever could.

6

Parker sat across from Shannon at one of the picnic tables outside the dining hall, sandwiches spread between them. The November sun warmed his back, and the lunch break was a welcome pause after spending the morning checking out the outdoor staging area on the far side of the property.

Shannon swept her long brown hair forward over one shoulder, a nervous habit he was starting to recognize.

"It's not what I had in mind," she said, pointing a potato chip at him. "I think the dining hall is the better venue."

"Agreed." Parker unwrapped his sandwich and bit off a hunk, watching her for a moment longer than necessary. Two days before, she'd had him arrested. Yesterday, they'd found a tentative working rhythm. Today, sitting across from her felt... better. "That pea gravel and tent setup works for casual events, but—"

"But it doesn't fit my idea of a gala for wealthy donors," she finished. She pulled out her tablet, pulling up photos she'd taken of the dining hall. "This space, though... The log beams, the windows, the fireplace. This is what will draw the donations we need."

"And Drake's already excited about coordinating the food," Parker added. "You won't get that level of service with a tent."

Shannon smiled. "Good. I'm glad we're on the same page."

His phone buzzed against the wooden table. Parker glanced at the screen, and his stomach dropped.

His attorney.

"Sorry," he said, setting down his sandwich. "I need to take this."

Shannon nodded, pulling her tablet closer to review the dining hall photos, giving him privacy while staying present.

Parker stood and walked a few paces away as he answered. "Mitchell."

"Parker. I have news about the garnishment case."

The attorney's tone told Parker everything he needed to know before the words came. Still, he listened as Mitchell laid it out in careful legal language that boiled down to one simple truth: the judge would not hear his appeal.

"Court's position is that we already got the judgment itself vacated, they will not spend resources on the restitution matter," Mitchell said. "You proved you're not Lucas, so you're not liable for future claims. But the money that was garnished from your wages at your previous job? They're calling that a civil matter between you and your former employer."

Parker paced back and forth, fighting the familiar burn of injustice. Two thousand dollars. Gone. Taken to pay for crimes Lucas committed, for debts Lucas owed, for damage Lucas caused.

"So that's it," he said flatly. "I just lost two grand to pay for something Lucas did."

"I'm sorry. I wish I had better news." Mitchell paused. "For what it's worth, you have a strong case against your brother for the identity theft itself. If we can ever locate him—"

"Don't bother." Parker cut him off. The words came out harsher than he intended, edged with the exhaustion of fighting battles he never started. "Lucas doesn't work. Doesn't own property. Has nothing of his own worth suing for. Even if you found him, I'd just be throwing good money after bad."

"I understand. I'll send you the final documentation. And Parker? I really am sorry."

After the call ended, Parker eased onto the bench across from Shannon again, setting his phone down on the table with more force than necessary. He stared at his half-eaten sandwich, appetite gone, jaw clenched against the anger building in his gut.

"Is everything okay?" Shannon's voice was concerned.

"No."

The word came out before he could stop it, raw and honest. He dragged a hand through his hair, not quite meeting her eyes.

Shannon set down her tablet. "What happened?"

"My attorney." Parker gestured vaguely with one hand, the motion sharp with frustration. "Lucas used my social security number when a court ruled against him. My previous employer garnished my wages—two thousand dollars total—before I even knew what was happening. Before I could prove I wasn't him."

"That's—" Shannon's brows pulled together. "That's not fair."

"No," he agreed quietly. "It's not."

"You're not Lucas." She said it as a fact, like something that required no debate or proof.

The tension in his neck lessened at those three words. "The judge won't hear my appeal. My attorney already got the actual judgment dropped. Proved I wasn't liable for Lucas's crimes. But the money that was already taken? They're calling it a civil matter between me and my former employer."

"That's ridiculous." Shannon's hands curled into fists on the table. "This is identity theft. There are laws—"

"Doesn't matter." The words came out flat, resigned. "I'd have to sue Lucas directly, and he has nothing. No property, no steady income, nothing worth going after that he didn't steal from someone else. I'd just waste more money trying to get it back."

She shook her head. "I know someone. A fantastic identity theft attorney in Phoenix. She specializes in cases like this—"

"Won't make a difference." Parker cut her off gently, appreciating the offer even though he knew it was pointless. "My attorney's good too. He already did what could be done. Got the actual judgment against me dropped, made sure Lucas's crimes won't show up on my record going forward. That's what matters."

"But your money—"

"Is gone." Parker heard the resignation in his own voice. "Two thousand dollars that I worked for. That I earned. Just... gone."

She reached across the table, her hand covering his briefly before withdrawing it. "I'm sorry. This isn't right. You shouldn't have to pay for what he did."

He looked at the spot where her hand had been, surprised by the gesture from the woman his brother had destroyed years ago. "At least I caught it when I did. Quit that job before they could take any more. It's taken months of working with Mitchell to even get this far. Getting the judgment itself dropped was huge. I should be grateful for that."

"You can be grateful for that and still be angry about losing two thousand dollars you earned. Both things can be true."

"Maybe." He studied her face, found those brown eyes watching him with something that looked like understanding. "What else can I do besides let it go? I could rage about it. Could obsess over the injustice. Could spend the next six months bitter and angry. But that just means Lucas wins twice. Once when he steals, once when I let it consume me."

"I hadn't thought about it that way." Shannon was quiet for a moment before she picked up her sandwich. "For what it's worth, I'm sorry this happened to you."

Parker picked up his sandwich, grateful to move on. But as they finished their lunch and talked through the afternoon's schedule, he caught her glancing at him with the same fierce protectiveness she'd shown when she first heard about the case.

She'd defended him without hesitation. Had called the situation unfair, had insisted he wasn't Lucas, had offered help even when he didn't accept it.

And somehow that mattered more than the two thousand dollars he'd lost.

———

SHANNON WATCHED PARKER pick up his sandwich again, his movements deliberate, controlled. But she saw the tension coiled in his shoulders, the way his jaw worked as he chewed like he was forcing himself to move past the conversation, to let it go.

Two thousand dollars. Gone. Taken to pay for crimes he didn't commit.

And he was just... accepting it.

The injustice of it twisted her stomach. She wanted to fix it, wanted to make that phone call to her contact in Phoenix, wanted to do something that would restore what Lucas had stolen. Her fingers twitched toward her phone before she caught herself.

No, that would be interfering. Overstepping. Parker had made his choice—to let it go, to refuse to let Lucas's crimes consume him—and she needed to respect that, even if every instinct screamed that he deserved better.

"You're thinking too loud," Parker said, with a hint of amusement in his voice despite everything.

Shannon blinked, realizing she'd been staring at him.

"Sorry. I just—" She shook her head. "It's not fair. None of it."

"No," he agreed. "But fair and reality don't always line up."

The resignation in his voice made her heart ache. How many times had he been through this? How many Lucas-sized craters had he learned to navigate, accepting losses that should never have been his to bear? She'd only had the one.

She parted her lips, ready to say more, but he focused on his sandwich again. Fine. She'd drop it.

"Hey there," Adan's voice carried across the patio. Shannon turned to see him approaching their table, his easy gait relaxed despite the work clothes and dust that clung to him. "Sorry to interrupt lunch, but I think I've got a solution to Shannon's office space problem."

She straightened, grateful for the interruption. "Office space?"

"You mentioned needing somewhere to spread out all your planning materials," Adan said, stopping beside their table. "Somewhere you could leave things set up without impacting daily operations. I think I've got just the spot, but it's gonna take a little muscle to clear it out."

Parker pushed back from the table, the shift from vulnerable to practical happening so smoothly Shannon almost missed it. Almost. But she caught the slight tension in his shoulders easing, caught the relief in his eyes.

"What did you have in mind?" Parker asked.

"Storage room off the dining hall." Adan gestured toward the building behind them. "It's full of junk and boxes right now. If we cleared it out, it'd be a decent space. Maybe a little cramped. But private enough for phone calls and planning."

Shannon's mind immediately started visualizing it. "The room with the view into the dining hall?"

"That's the one." Adan grinned.

"That sounds perfect," Shannon said, already making mental notes about table placement, filing systems, how she'd organize vendor contacts and auction materials.

"Only problem is it's packed floor to ceiling with stuff that needs moving," Adan continued. "Tables, chairs, old decorations, things we haven't touched in years. Gonna take some work to clear it out."

"I can help," Parker said immediately.

"Me too," she added. "It's my office space. I should help set it up."

Adan's eyes crinkled with amusement. "Alright then. Let's go look at what we're working with."

As they gathered their lunch trash and headed toward the dining hall, Shannon walked beside Parker. Their arms brushed, and she was acutely aware of the shift between them since that phone call. She'd defended him without thinking, had insisted he wasn't Lucas with a fierce certainty that surprised even her.

And he'd let her see his vulnerability, had trusted her with his frustration and his choice to let it go.

The guilt she'd been carrying since the arrest — since the moment she'd realized her mistake — felt lighter now. Not gone entirely, but loosening its grip.

Parker held the door open for her, and as Shannon passed him, their eyes met. She looked away as her pulse thrummed.

"Thank you," he said quietly.

"Always."

Then Adan called them toward the storage room, and the moment broke. But as Shannon followed the two men deeper into the dining hall, she realized the weight she'd been dragging around had shifted into something else. Purpose, maybe. Or the beginning of trust.

They had work to do and an office to set up. And for the first time since this whole mess started, she was glad to be doing it alongside Parker.

7

SHANNON PULLED INTO the Vargas Ranch parking lot earlier than necessary. She'd told Parker nine o'clock, but anticipation had her awake and dressed by five-thirty, packed, and ready for her day.

Through the barn's open doors, she spotted him leading a chestnut gelding toward the pasture. She watched him check the horse's legs before releasing it. The crisp morning air carried the soft cooing of desert quail across the open land.

"Morning!" she called.

He looked up, blinking at her early arrival. Then he smiled, a warm smile lighting his blue eyes. "Hey. Just getting started with turnout. Give me about ten minutes."

She could wait at his truck. That would be the professional thing to do. Stay out of his way, letting him finish his morning routine. After working beside Parker for a week, she didn't feel right about sitting on the sidelines.

"Can I help? I don't mind."

He studied her for a moment, and Shannon suddenly wondered if her cream blouse and dark jeans were too dressed up for barn work.

"You sure? These guys can be a little pushy if they think you've got treats."

"I can handle pushy horses. I spent plenty of time

around them growing up."

His eyebrows raised. "Alright then. Want to grab Sage? She's in the fourth stall down."

Shannon entered the barn, breathing in the scents of hay, leather, and horse. The bay mare in the fourth stall nickered as she approached.

"Hey there, beautiful." Shannon lifted the halter, and Sage lowered her head cooperatively. She remembered the motions even after years away from regular horse handling during those summers at Aunt Shirley's, finding peace in the stables when home felt too empty.

She'd forgotten how much she missed this.

Parker waited by the gate, watching her approach with Sage.

"She likes you."

"I like her too. She's got kind eyes." Shannon glanced at him as they walked. "How long have you been working with horses?"

"Since I was a kid. Dad had me on a miniature pony by five or six. Said if I was going to live on a ranch, I needed to understand the animals that made it run."

"Your dad sounds like a wise man."

"He was." His voice went quiet. "He would have liked this place. The Vargas family reminds me of him. People who understand taking care of the land and animals comes first."

They reached the gate, and he held it while Shannon led Sage through. The mare headed straight for the water trough, and Shannon released her with a pat.

Walking back toward the barn, something settled in her heart. A rightness.

Their boots crunched in rhythm on the gravel, falling into step without trying. After one week of working together, they already had a rhythm.

"So," she said, taking a risk, "do you follow basketball at all?"

Parker stopped so abruptly she took two more steps before realizing it. She turned back. He stared at her with wide eyes. "Basketball?"

"Yeah. I know you're more of a ranch guy, but I was curious."

A laugh escaped him. "Shannon, I've been a Phoenix Suns fan since I was eight years old. My dad and I used to listen to games on the radio while we worked."

"No way! Really?"

"Really. Why are you..." He paused, studying her face. "Wait. Are you telling me you're a basketball fan?"

"Lifelong Suns fan." Shannon pulled out her phone, fingers trembling slightly. She'd never expected they would share a love of basketball. Lucas had found it annoying. "Want to see something incredible?"

She scrolled to her saved videos, aware of her shoulder brushing his arm as she angled the screen. "Here. Deandre Ayton's dunk against Dallas."

They watched Ayton soar over three defenders.

"That's incredible," he breathed. "Look at the elevation. I've watched that highlight probably twenty times."

"Only twenty?" Shannon grinned up at him. "I've got it bookmarked. Sometimes I watch it when I need to remember what determination looks like."

"Your dad got you into basketball?" He led the last horse from its stall, a gray gelding with a white blaze.

"My great-aunt, actually. Aunt Shirley had season tickets for years, lower bowl behind the bench." A touch of sadness laced her words. She missed those tickets and spending time with her great-aunt. "Some of my best childhood memories are of those games. We'd drive down together, stop at this little Italian place she loved, then head to the arena early enough to watch warmups. She taught me player stats, game strategy, everything. Made me fall completely in love with basketball."

"Sounds like she was pretty special." His voice carried

genuine interest as he clipped the lead rope onto the gelding's halter.

"She is. Still is." Shannon latched the stall door before catching up with him. "After my mom left when I was twelve, Aunt Shirley stepped in. Gave me a place to belong, things to look forward to. Those basketball games were our time together, just the two of us, cheering for our team."

He glanced at her as they walked the gelding toward the pasture. "What happened to the season tickets?"

Shannon hesitated. They'd worked together for a week now, built an easy rapport planning the gala and coordinating charity details. But this felt different. More personal. More vulnerable. Still, he knew what Lucas had done to her. Knew his twin had stolen from her, destroying her trust. And Parker had been nothing but respectful about it, never making excuses.

"I had to sell them." She kept her eyes on the gelding's smooth gait as they walked outside. "After Lucas took my money. I had tuition bills coming due, rent to pay. The tickets were worth something, so..." She shrugged, trying for casual and not quite achieving it. "They had to go."

He stopped walking. When Shannon glanced at him, something raw flickered across his face. Pain, anger, and guilt all mixed together.

"Shannon, I'm —"

"You don't need to apologize." She cut him off gently but firmly. "You didn't steal from me. Lucas did. You're not responsible for his choices."

"No, but..." His jaw tightened. "Those tickets were important to you. And he took that from you along with everything else."

The understanding in his voice, the way he grasped what the loss had cost her beyond dollars, made Shannon's throat tighten.

"Yeah," she whispered. "He did. But I'm working on forgiving him for it. Working on not letting what he took define what I still have."

They reached the gate, and she held it while Parker un-clipped the gelding. The horse trotted off to join his pasture mates, and for a moment they both watched him go, the morning sun climbing higher and warming the surrounding air.

"For what it's worth," he said, his voice low, "you shouldn't have had to give those up because of my brother."

Shannon turned to face him fully. His gaze held hers, and the air between them seemed to still. When her cheeks warmed, she looked away, her pulse unsteady.

"Thank you," she whispered.

Parker cleared his throat and fell into step beside her, their boots clomping on the packed dirt as they walked back to the barn.

An idea sparked. Mischievous and wonderful. She'd been nervous about the Phoenix trip, worried about how they'd fill the drive time, whether the easy rapport they'd built at the ranch would translate to hours in a truck togeth-er. But this changed everything. This shared love of basket-ball made what she had planned even better.

She glanced sideways at him, barely containing her smile. "So, since you love basketball so much, you're abso-lutely going to love our first donor stop today."

His steps slowed. "What do you mean?"

"Can't tell you. It's a surprise." She nudged his shoulder and smiled, knowing she was about to give him a wonderful gift that had nothing to do with the past and everything to do with this new friendship. "But trust me. You're going to want to bring your phone for pictures."

"Shannon." Parker stopped walking entirely, turning to face her with an expression caught between hope and disbe-lief. "Where are we going?"

"You'll find out in about an hour." She grinned at him, lighter than she had been in days. "Come on, let's get these guys finished so we can hit the road. We've got a schedule to keep."

He shook his head, but he was smiling now too. "You're really not going to tell me?"

"Nope. Where's the fun in that?" Shannon headed toward the barn, calling over her shoulder. "Besides, some things are better as surprises. Trust me on this one."

He laughed behind her, a sound that sent warmth rippling through her. They'd built the beginnings of real friendship. Maybe more than friendship, if she was honest with herself. The way her pulse jumped when he smiled at her, the way she looked for excuses to be near him, the way his understanding about the season tickets had made her want to tell him.

Dangerous territory. She knew that. Parker carried the same appearance as the man who had lied to her and betrayed her trust. Every logical part of her brain screamed caution.

But Parker deserved to be seen for who he was, not judged by his brother's crimes. And today, on this trip to Phoenix, she was going to show him she saw him. Not as Lucas's twin, but as Parker Quaid. A man who loved basketball and his father's memory, who treated horses with gentle respect, and who understood loss.

The thought made her nervous and excited in equal measure.

"Hey Shannon?" he called as she reached the barn door.

She turned back. "Yeah?"

He held her gaze for a moment, something unguarded in his expression. "Thanks for helping with turnout."

Her heart gave a small, traitorous skip. "Of course."

She ducked into the barn before the moment could get too heavy, but she couldn't quite wipe the smile off her face as they finished up and headed toward his truck.

If her surprise went the way she hoped, Parker Quaid was about to have a morning he'd never forget.

———

The Phoenix Suns facility. They were going to the Suns facility. In person. Him.

Parker's hands tightened on the steering wheel as the Phoenix skyline grew larger on the horizon, the drive from Wickenburg melting away behind them. Shannon sat in the passenger seat, her excitement evident in the way she kept checking her watch and reviewing notes on her tablet, but he was only half-listening to her explain the donation strategy for the gala.

"You're quiet," Shannon observed, glancing over at him with a small smile. "Nervous about meeting donors?"

"Something like that," he managed, not quite ready to admit how much this visit meant to him.

Dad had been gone for three years now, but basketball kept him alive somehow. Every game Parker watched felt like a conversation they were still having.

How could he explain to Shannon that basketball wasn't just an interest? It was the thread that connected him to the best memories of his father, to a time before Lucas's crimes had stolen everything good from the Quaid family name.

The training building rose from the desert like something out of a dream he'd never dared to have. Glass and steel gleamed in the afternoon light, the team logo etched into the facade like a promise of everything that happened inside.

He whistled low as they pulled into the visitor lot. "This is where they practice?"

"State of the art," Shannon confirmed, checking her watch. "Wait until you see the inside."

She reached for her portfolio in the back seat, but Parker stayed still, staring at the building. Somewhere inside, players he'd watched for decades were running drills, perfecting their craft, preparing for games that brought joy to thousands. Including him. Including Dad. Before everything fell apart.

"You okay?" Shannon asked gently.

"Yeah, just..." Parker forced himself to release his grip on the steering wheel. "I've been following this team for twenty years, and I never imagined I'd actually be here."

"Well, come on then." The brightness in her eyes made his heart race in ways that had nothing to do with the Suns facility. "Let me introduce you to some people."

He donned his cowboy hat and followed her inside.

The lobby exceeded anything Parker could have imagined. Soaring ceilings stretched three stories high; the space flooded with natural light from floor-to-ceiling windows. The walls were lined with photographs chronicling the team's entire history — championship moments, legendary players, fans celebrating in the streets of Phoenix after playoff victories.

"That's what we're hoping to be part of," Shannon said, coming to stand beside him as he studied a display of the team's community outreach programs. Photos of players visiting children's hospitals, and hosting camps for underprivileged kids. "The Suns have always used their platform to support the community. That's why Marcus was so interested when I contacted him about Braden's Hope."

"Ms. Burke!"

Parker turned to see a tall, distinguished man approaching with a smile that immediately put people at ease. Mid-fifties, graying temples, wearing a team polo that looked both professional and approachable.

"Marcus, so good to see you," Shannon said, stepping forward for a brief handshake. "Thank you again for making time for us today. This is Parker Quaid. He works at Vargas Ranch with the equine therapy program."

"Parker, pleasure to meet you." Marcus extended his hand with genuine warmth. "Shannon has told me incredible things about what you're doing with disabled children and veterans. That's exactly the innovative approach we want to support."

Parker shook his hand, grateful his voice came out steady. "It's an honor to be here, sir. I've been a Suns fan for as long as I can remember."

"A loyal fan." Marcus's approval was evident. "Those are the best kind. Come on, let me show you around before we talk business."

The next hour passed in a blur of wonders that Parker knew he'd replay in his mind for years. Marcus showed them championship-level practice courts that gleamed under overhead lights, weight rooms filled with cutting-edge equipment, and world-class training facilities.

But what struck Parker most wasn't the technology or the expensive equipment. It was the sound—the rhythmic bounce of basketballs echoing through the court, and the squeak of shoes on hardwood, voices calling out plays. The facility was alive with the game he loved, and every nerve in his body sang with the recognition of being somewhere he belonged.

They continued the tour, Marcus pointing out the community partnerships wall, the players' lounge, and the medical facilities that kept athletes healthy.

They were heading back toward the main corridor when Marcus checked his watch and smiled. "Perfect timing. We have time for you to meet some players if you'd like."

Parker's heart stopped. He couldn't speak.

Shannon smiled, mischievousness glinting in her eyes. "I think that would mean a lot to Parker."

Marcus's smile widened. "Given what you're doing for these kids with Braden's Hope, I'd like to make this afternoon memorable for both of you."

Meeting actual NBA players felt surreal in ways Parker's brain was still struggling to process. These were men he'd watched on television for years, studied and admired from the distance of a screen. And now, they were right in front of him. Taller than they looked on TV, more muscular, but with regular faces and normal expressions that reminded him they were human beings who just happened to be extraordinarily gifted at basketball.

Marcus made introductions, explaining about Braden's Hope and the work being done with equine therapy. The players leaned in, asking thoughtful questions about the program that Shannon answered with passionate expertise. One pulled out his phone to take notes. Another asked her to repeat the website address.

"Parker's the one who works directly with the horses," Shannon said, and suddenly three pairs of professional athlete eyes were focused on him. "He's been working with them his whole life."

"What's that like?" one player asked. "Working with horses has to be completely different from working with people."

Parker found his voice, relying on years of ranch experience to calm his nerves. "Horses are honest. They don't lie; they don't have hidden agendas. You're confident and clear in your handling, or you're not. Kids learn fast that pretending doesn't work. Horses see right through it."

"That's deep," another player said thoughtfully. "Kind of like basketball. You can't fake hustle, can't pretend to care about the game. It shows up in how you play."

And just like that, Parker was having an actual conversation about work, passion, and the ways different activities could teach the same life lessons. The players weren't performing for cameras. They were just guys talking shop with someone who understood dedication and craft in a different context.

When Marcus mentioned getting photos for the charity's promotional materials, the players agreed immediately. Shannon directed Parker to stand with them, and he was sandwiched between professional athletes, their arms around his shoulders like they were teammates.

After the photos, one player grabbed a basketball. "You

said you played in high school? Let's see what you've got."

The next few minutes were the most surreal of Parker's life. He was on an NBA practice court, running simple plays with professional players, the muscle memory of the game overriding his nervousness. His first shots missed—adrenaline making his touch too strong—but then one felt right. The ball left his fingers with proper rotation and swished through the net with a sound that sent electricity down his spine.

"There it is!" one player called out. "Money shot!"

They ran a few more plays before Marcus called time. As the players headed back to their regular practice, each one shook Parker's hand with genuine smiles.

"Good luck with the charity," one said. "What you're doing is important. Keep at it."

After they said their goodbyes and Marcus led them back toward the lobby, Parker couldn't stop grinning. He'd met NBA players. Had actual conversations with them. Shot baskets on their practice court.

Marcus returned with a large shopping bag bearing the Suns logo. "Shannon, here are the items we discussed for your auction. Courtside Christmas Day tickets, two additional regular season games, signed jerseys from several players, team merchandise, and a basketball autographed by the entire roster."

He handed the bag to Shannon, then turned to Parker. "It was a pleasure meeting you."

They shook hands one more time, and Parker thanked him properly, though the gratitude felt inadequate for the gift he'd been given.

As they walked back toward the truck, Parker's legs felt unsteady. Underneath the excitement, something deeper churned. Something that made his throat tight and his eyes sting.

Shannon walked beside him in silence, and he was grateful for the space to breathe and try to organize his scattered thoughts.

When they reached the truck, Parker leaned against the driver's door for a moment, his hands still shaking slightly. Shannon set the shopping bag carefully in the back seat, then came to stand beside him. She said nothing. Just waited, her presence steady and patient.

Parker swallowed hard, staring at the Suns facility gleaming in the afternoon light. "My dad would have loved this."

The words came out rougher than he intended, thick with emotion he hadn't meant to show.

"Tell me about him," Shannon whispered.

Parker's chest tightened. "He got me into basketball. We didn't have cable growing up, so we'd listen to games together on this old portable radio while we worked the ranch. He'd be fixing fences or mucking stalls, and I'd be right there beside him, and we'd have the game on. Even when we couldn't see it, we followed every play."

"That sounds special."

"It was." Parker's throat worked. "Basketball wasn't just a game to us. It was... our thing. Dad would explain the plays, helping me understand what made them work. He always said basketball was a thinking man's game. That every possession told a story."

Shannon's fingers found his hand, warm and steady.

"On special occasions," Parker continued, the memories flooding back now, "when we'd had a good week at the ranch or sold cattle for better than expected, Dad would take me to Murphy's Bar in Flagstaff. We'd sit at the counter, splitting an order of wings, watching the Suns on the big screen. The other regulars knew us by name, saved us seats during playoff runs." His voice cracked. "Dad always said if we ever got the chance to go to a real game, we'd sit courtside or not at all."

He immediately regretted how that sounded. But Shannon just squeezed his hand, her eyes soft with understanding.

"He passed three years ago," Parker managed. "Every game I watch feels like he's right there with me."

He paused, forcing himself to be honest. "Lucas's crimes didn't just destroy our family's reputation. They destroyed Dad. The stress, the shame, trying to fix what couldn't be fixed. It broke him."

"Oh, Parker."

"But today..." Parker turned to look at her fully, this woman who'd been so wronged by his brother but had seen Parker as his own person with his own dreams and losses and passions. "Today, being here, meeting those players, standing on that court. It felt like I got something back. Something I thought was gone forever."

"What's that?" Shannon asked, her voice barely above a whisper.

"The ability to believe good things can happen to me too." His voice came out rough, honest. "That I can have dreams that aren't just about avoiding Lucas's messes or taking care of other people. That I can want something for myself and maybe—" He swallowed hard. "Maybe actually get it."

Shannon grabbed both his hands in hers. They felt warm and soft against his work-roughened hands. Delicate and comforting. His throat tightened when she squeezed them as she spoke. "Sometimes we have to let ourselves receive the blessings God offers us."

They stood there in the parking lot, the Phoenix afternoon sun warm on their shoulders, the Suns facility gleaming behind them like a promise kept. Something fundamental had shifted inside him. Maybe he could be the man Shannon saw when she looked at him. Not Lucas's twin. Just Parker.

"Thank you," he said finally, his voice thick. "For this. For giving me back something I didn't even realize I'd lost."

Shannon's smile was tremulous, her own eyes bright

with unshed tears. "You're welcome."

As they climbed into the truck and pulled out of the parking lot, Shannon chattered excitedly about the auction items and how much money they'd raise. Parker let himself smile, a quiet joy settling into places that had been empty for too long.

Trust me on this one, she'd said that morning, her eyes bright with a secret.

She'd delivered on her promise with a day he'd be telling his grandkids about.

8

THE PHOENIX SKYLINE shrank in the rearview mirror as Parker guided the truck back onto US 60, heading west toward Wickenburg. Beside him, Shannon reviewed the donation paperwork Marcus had provided, calculating auction values and making notes on her tablet. Professional. Focused.

Then she'd glance at the Suns-branded shopping bag in the back seat, and that small smile would appear. She'd try to hide it, ducking her head back to her tablet, but Parker caught it every time.

The desert stretched ahead, endless and familiar, dotted with saguaro cacti standing like sentinels against the pale November sky. The sun hung lower now, painting everything in warm gold that would deepen to amber as they drove. This part of Arizona felt different from Flagstaff. Wide open. Impossible to hide in.

Maybe that's why the words came easier than they should have.

"That radio in the barn," Parker started, then stopped. He didn't know why he was telling her this. "It was so old the reception cut out half the time. Dad would fiddle with it between quarters, trying to get it to work. But we'd listen anyway."

Shannon stayed quiet. Waiting.

"When he got sick—" Parker's throat tightened. He forced the words out. "Cancer. The treatments didn't work. Basketball was the only normal thing left. We'd argue about roster moves, debate coaching strategies. Anything not to talk about him dying."

Shannon reached across the center console and rested her hand on his forearm. The warmth seeped through his sleeve. He wanted to cover it with his own, but didn't.

"He passed away three years ago." Parker kept his eyes on the road. "Heart attack. Two weeks after the final medical bills came. The stress of everything—the cancer, the debt, Lucas's latest arrest. His heart just... gave out."

"Oh, Parker." Shannon's voice carried genuine grief. "I'm so sorry."

"The worst part?" He forced himself to push through the pain he usually kept carefully locked away. "I left the day after his funeral because Lucas had people looking for him, and they didn't much care about the difference between us. Mom said it would be better if I made myself scarce until things cooled down. So I left her alone to deal with everything—the bills, the ranch, the grief. Left her when she needed me most."

"That wasn't your choice," Shannon said firmly. "That was Lucas's crimes forcing you out."

"Doesn't make it easier." Parker's hands flexed on the steering wheel. "I send money when I can, but it's not the same as being there. It's not the same as helping her run that ranch, or sitting with her on the hard days when she misses him so much she can barely breathe."

They drove in silence for several miles, the desert unchanging around them. But the quiet wasn't uncomfortable. It felt like Shannon was giving him space to let the grief breathe instead of shoving it back down where it usually lived.

"Today at the facility," Parker finally said, "all I could think was how much Dad would have loved it."

"He would have," Shannon agreed. "But Parker, I think he'd be just as happy knowing you got to experience it. That you're still following the team you loved together, that basketball is still part of your life."

"You really think so?"

"I know so." Shannon's voice carried absolute certainty. "Parents don't stop wanting good things for their children just because they're gone. Your father would want you to have dreams, to experience joy, to build a life that isn't defined by Lucas's crimes. He'd want you to be happy."

The words settled over Parker. Maybe Shannon was right. Maybe honoring his father's memory didn't mean sacrificing his own happiness out of guilt for surviving when Dad didn't. Maybe the best way to honor that relationship was to keep loving basketball, to keep following the Suns, to let joy back into his life instead of holding it at arm's length.

"Thank you," he said again, but this time the words carried a different weight. "For understanding."

"Of course." Shannon's hand squeezed his arm gently before releasing. "Family is complicated, especially when we lose them too soon. The grief doesn't ever really go away. We just learn to carry it differently."

Something in her tone made Parker glance over, catching sympathy mixed with understanding.

"You sound like you're speaking from experience," he said carefully, not wanting to push but suddenly curious about the shadows in her eyes.

Shannon was quiet for so long that Parker thought she might not answer. She turned back toward the window, watching the desert roll past, and he was about to apologize for prying when she spoke.

"My mother left when I was twelve."

The words were simple, matter-of-fact, but Parker heard the hurt underneath them.

"Left?"

"Just... left." Shannon's laugh was short and bitter. "No

warning, no explanation that made sense to a twelve-year-old girl. One day she was there, complaining about the Arizona heat and my father's work schedule. The next day she was gone. Packed two suitcases and walked out while I was at school."

Something protective flared in him for twelve-year-old Shannon, abandoned without explanation or goodbye. "That's—Shannon, I'm so sorry."

"My father tried to explain it. Said she wasn't happy, that Arizona wasn't what she'd expected when they moved here for his work, that she needed to find herself or some other excuse that sounded reasonable to adults but made no sense to a kid." Shannon's voice stayed even, controlled, but her hands twisted together in her lap. "What I heard was that I wasn't enough reason for her to stay."

"That's not—" Parker started, but Shannon shook her head.

"I know. Logically, I know it wasn't about me. She left my father. Left his workaholic lifestyle. I was just... collateral damage in her search for whatever she thought she was missing." Shannon took a shaky breath. "But twelve-year-old me didn't understand her reasons. I just understood that my mother looked at her life—at me—and decided it wasn't worth staying for."

Parker reached across the console and caught her hand.

"Where's your father in all this?" he asked.

"Working." Shannon's smile was sad. "Jeff Burke is a good man. A brilliant man, actually—mining operations manager, respected in his field, and provides well. But he's emotionally... absent. Always has been, but after Mom left, he threw himself even deeper into work. I think it was easier for him to solve problems at the mine than to deal with his daughter's grief."

"So you dealt with it alone."

"Not entirely." Genuine warmth crept into her voice for the first time since this conversation started. "That's when

Aunt Shirley stepped in. My great-aunt on my mother's side, still living in Wickenburg where she'd been for decades. She'd been peripherally involved in my life before — birthday cards, occasional visits — but after Mom left, she became my lifeline."

Parker remembered what Shannon had said at the ranch, about spending winters and holidays in Wickenburg. "She took you in?"

"Every chance she could." Shannon's smile was real now. "Dad would bring me to stay with her during school breaks, summer vacations, any time he had to travel for work. Aunt Shirley's house became my sanctuary. She taught me to ride horses, took me to rodeos and concerts, let me just be a kid without the weight of wondering why I wasn't enough for my mother."

"She sounds incredible."

"She is." Shannon's voice carried fierce love. "Aunt Shirley showed me what it meant to be chosen, to have someone actively want you in their life. She didn't have to step up for me. I wasn't her responsibility. But she chose to be the maternal figure I needed, to give me stability and love and a place where I felt wanted."

The pieces clicked. That's why Shannon did this — the charity work, showing up for people, making things happen for kids who needed someone to choose them. Because Shirley had chosen her.

"That's why the charity work matters so much to you," he said. "You're paying forward what she gave you."

"Maybe." Shannon seemed to consider this. "Or maybe I just learned from the best. Aunt Shirley taught me that choosing to invest in people — really invest, not just surface-level support — can change their entire trajectory. She did that for me when I was twelve and adrift. Now I get to do it for others."

They approached the Wickenburg turnoff now, the familiar landscape of his new home rising around them. But

Parker didn't want this conversation to end, didn't want to lose this moment of vulnerability and understanding that had opened between them.

"What about your mom?" he asked. "Do you still have contact with her?"

Shannon shook her head. "Birthday cards the first few years, then those stopped too. Last I heard, she was living in Oregon with a new husband and stepkids. She tried to reach out a few years ago—I was finishing college—but I wasn't ready. Maybe I'm still not ready. I don't know."

"That's okay," Parker said firmly. "You get to decide what healing looks like. Nobody gets to tell you how to feel about being abandoned."

"You understand that. The complexity of family hurt."

"Yeah." Parker thought about his own mother, about the years of feeling second best to Lucas, about the complicated grief of loving someone who couldn't quite see you clearly. "Family is supposed to be the people who know you best and love you anyway. But sometimes they're the ones who hurt us deepest because we need them so much."

"Exactly." Shannon's voice was soft. "And then people like Aunt Shirley come along and remind us what it's supposed to look like. What it means to be chosen, to be seen, to be valued just for who you are."

They pulled into the Vargas Ranch parking lot, the main buildings silhouetted against the late afternoon sky. Parker put the truck in park but didn't move to get out, and Shannon stayed still beside him, both of them reluctant to end this moment of raw honesty.

"Thank you for telling me about your mom," Parker said. "For trusting me with that."

"Thank you for telling me about your dad." Shannon squeezed his hand.

They sat in the truck as the desert light faded into evening, the silence between them comfortable and full of understanding. Parker realized that something had fundamentally changed during this drive. They'd moved past professional courtesy and tentative friendship into something deeper.

They were both survivors. Both healing. Both learning to believe that good things could happen to them despite everything that had tried to convince them otherwise.

"I should let you get to your work," Shannon said finally, though she didn't sound eager to leave. "I know you have evening chores, and I have about a hundred gala details to finalize."

"Right." Parker loosened his grip on her hand, though every instinct told him not to. "But Shannon?"

She paused, one hand on the door handle, and looked back at him.

He forced himself to meet her eyes, to let her see the truth he was still learning to accept. "Today, you saw what mattered to me, and you made it happen. That's —" He coughed. "That means everything."

Shannon blinked rapidly, looking away for a moment before meeting his gaze again. "You deserve to be seen, Parker. You don't have to earn every good thing that happens. Sometimes you can just... receive them."

"I'm trying," he admitted. "You're making it easier to try."

She smiled, then climbed out of the truck before either of them could say something that might push this moment into territory neither was quite ready for. Parker watched her walk toward her car, the Suns donation bag carefully cradled in her arms. The setting sun caught in her hair.

He should probably be worried about how much he wanted her to stay.

———

SHANNON STARED AT the dining hall layout diagram spread across the folding table, her pencil tapping an irritated rhythm against the paper. The converted storage room smelled faintly of dust and old wood despite their best cleaning efforts two weeks ago, but the space served its purpose—a dedicated planning hub tucked just off the main dining hall where she could spread out vendor contracts, seating charts, and auction item lists without worrying about disturbing ranch operations.

Through the open doorway, she had a clear view of Drake's coffee shop across the dining hall. The morning sun caught the dining hall windows just right, making them sparkle. She'd been here since six-thirty, trying to solve the puzzle of fitting eight more guests than originally planned into a space that already felt tight.

"Morning."

Shannon's head snapped up. Parker stood in the doorway, two cups from Drake's coffee shop in his hands. He wore his usual work clothes—jeans, boots, a flannel shirt rolled to his elbows—and his cowboy hat. Her pulse skipped a beat as a smile lit his blue eyes.

"I saw your car in the lot and figured you'd been here awhile." He crossed the small space in two strides and set one cup in front of her. "Medium vanilla latte, extra shot, light on the foam."

Her fingers brushed his as she reached for the cup, and warmth spread up her arm that had nothing to do with the coffee's temperature. "You remembered."

"You've ordered the same thing every morning for two weeks." His eyes held hers for a beat longer than necessary. "Hard not to notice."

Shannon wrapped both hands around the cup, using it as an excuse to look away from the intensity in his gaze. He'd remembered. Not just that she drank lattes, but the specific way she ordered them. Lucas had never remembered her coffee order, even after six months together.

She pushed the thought away and took a sip. Perfect temperature, perfect sweetness. "Thank you. I needed this."

"Rough morning already?" Parker pulled one of the

metal folding chairs around to her side of the table and sat, his shoulder a few inches from hers.

"Just trying to figure out how to fit more people into a space that's already at capacity." She gestured at the diagram with her free hand. "We've had eight more RSVPs come in, and I can't turn away potential donors."

Parker leaned forward, studying the layout. The movement brought him closer, and Shannon caught the scent of his aftershave—something woodsy and clean that made her want to breathe deeper. The air thickened. She forced her eyes onto the diagram, despite her racing heart.

"What if you moved these tables here?" His finger traced a line across the paper, and she leaned in to follow his logic, her hair slipping over her shoulder. When it brushed against his hand, he paused, his breath catching.

As she hurriedly swept her hair to the other side, her fingers grazed his arm. The warmth spread from the contact, and she wondered if he felt it too.

"Instead, scoot them over here. You'd open up that corner by the windows."

Shannon tilted her head, visualizing it. Their shoulders pressed together as they both bent over the table. "That could work, but then the sightlines to the stage might feel awkward for the people on the far side."

"Not if you shift the stage six feet to the left." When Parker pointed to it, his arm brushed hers. "See? Everyone would have a clear view, and you'd have room for at least two more round tables in the space you just created."

She grabbed a pencil and started sketching the change, acutely aware of how close he was, how the small room seemed to shrink around them. How right it felt being this close to him.

Forcing herself to concentrate on the task at hand, she finally said, "Parker, that's brilliant. Why didn't I see that?"

"Fresh eyes." His voice had gone quieter. "You've been staring at this for too long. Sometimes you just need someone to look at it differently."

Shannon set down her pencil and turned her head to thank him, only to realize how near he was. Close enough to see the lighter flecks of blue in his eyes. Close enough to count the days since he'd shaved. Her breath caught.

Two weeks had passed since the Suns' visit, since she'd watched his face glow with pure joy when those players walked in. Two weeks since he'd opened up about his father, his voice roughening on certain words, his guard dropping enough to let her see the man beneath the cowboy exterior. Even now, warmth spread through her at the memory.

Lucas had never shared like that. Never sent money home to help his mother. Never opened up about the people he loved or the work that mattered to him.

Parker did all of it without thinking twice.

The realization should have terrified her. Instead, it settled into a corner of her heart like something inevitable.

Then Parker's gaze dropped to her mouth for just a fraction of a second before snapping back up. "Shannon—"

"The extra tables," she said quickly, her voice coming out breathier than intended. "Where would you put them?"

He blinked, then cleared his throat and turned back to the diagram, putting a few crucial inches of space between them. "Right. Um. Here, maybe?" His finger pointed to a spot near the entrance. "Easy access for late arrivals, and it doesn't block the flow to the silent auction area."

Shannon forced herself to focus on the layout, on the practical problem in front of her rather than the way her skin still tingled where his arm had touched hers. She picked up the pencil again and sketched additional tables. "Perfect. That gives us room for sixteen more people if we need it."

"Always good to have a buffer." Parker leaned back in his chair, and Shannon felt the loss of his warmth like a physical thing.

They sat in silence, broken only by the faint clatter of dishes from the dining hall next door. Shannon took another sip of her coffee, hyperaware of Parker's presence beside her, of the way he'd known exactly what she needed this morning without her having to ask.

"So." Parker's voice broke the quiet. "What else is on your impossible list for today?"

She laughed despite herself. "It's not impossible. Just... ambitious."

"That's what I like about you." The words came out sincerely, and when Shannon met his eyes, she found him watching her with an expression she was too afraid to name. "You do nothing halfway."

"I should probably—" She gestured vaguely at the diagram, at the stacks of papers surrounding them, at anything that wasn't the way he was looking at her.

"Right. Yeah." Parker stood, the scrape of his chair against the concrete floor loud in the small space. "I've got some fence repairs Adan wanted me to check on this morning. But if you need anything else, just text me. I can swing back this afternoon."

"I'd like that." Her voice softened, warmth rising to her cheeks.

He paused in the doorway, one hand on the frame, backlit by the morning sun streaming through the dining hall. "Thanks for the coffee talk."

"You brought the coffee," Shannon pointed out, managing a smile.

"Yeah, but you made it worth the trip." He flashed her a grin that did dangerous things to her equilibrium, then headed out.

Shannon watched him go, her fingers still wrapped around the coffee cup he'd brought her. She could still smell the faint trace of his woodsy aftershave in the small room, could still feel the ghost of his arm against hers.

This was trouble. Her racing pulse had nothing to do with caffeine and everything to do with the man who'd shown up just to help.

Shannon placed her coffee on the table and pressed both palms flat against it, trying to ground herself. She had work to do. A gala to finish planning. Eight more guests to accommodate thanks to Parker's clever table arrangement.

She absolutely could not afford to think about the way his shoulder had felt pressed against hers, or how the room had gone silent and charged when their eyes met, or how she'd wanted to lean closer instead of pulling away.

Or how for half a second she wondered if he wanted to kiss her.

Or what she would have done had he tried.

She absolutely could not afford to think about any of it. But her fingers drifted to her lips anyway, and she wondered what his kiss would taste like. If it would be gentle or urgent, patient or passionate. If it would feel like coming home.

9

SHANNON MERGED FROM I-17 North onto the 74 West, tightening her grip on the steering wheel. The drive from her North Phoenix apartment to Vargas Ranch took an hour and fifteen minutes each way—a route she'd traveled daily for weeks through urban sprawl to wide open desert. Her favorite part was once she left the city behind. Beautiful mountains morphed from hues of blue into purple, rust, and finally gold the closer she came to the ranch.

Saguaro cacti stood, arms raised in eternal salute to the sun climbing steadily overhead. She'd made this drive enough times now that the scenery provided meditation, a transition space between her city life and the work that was quickly becoming the most important thing she'd ever done.

Her phone buzzed against the cup holder, and Shannon glanced at the caller ID before answering through the car's Bluetooth system.

"Morning, Aunt Shirley."

"Good morning, sweetheart. How are you holding up? You sound tired."

Her great-aunt's voice steadied her the way the morning sun warmed the desert. The same voice that had talked her through geometry homework, through her mother's abandonment, through late-night phone calls during college, and through every painful day after Lucas.

"I'm fine. Just driving to the ranch."

"Ah yes, the charity event you've been pouring your heart into. How's that coming along?"

"Better than I dared hope." Excitement crept into her voice as she passed a truck loaded with hay bales. "We've got confirmations from some major donors, and the venue is going to be absolutely perfect."

"And how are things going with your coworkers? Dylan and Adan seem like good men from what you've told me."

"They are. They really are." Shannon slowed slightly as traffic thickened near an exit. "They've been incredibly supportive, and they genuinely care about the kids this program serves. I'm glad to work with people motivated by the mission and not profit margins. I couldn't picture myself working in the corporate world."

"Neither could I. What about the cowboy? Parker, wasn't it? The one you had that unfortunate misunderstanding with on your first day."

Shannon's pulse quickened at the mention of Parker's name, and she was grateful Aunt Shirley couldn't see the flush climbing her neck. "Parker... he's been great to work with."

"Just great?" Her aunt's tone held a touch of amusement, like someone who had spent years deciphering emotions hidden in the subtleties of human speech. "You've worked closely together for nearly a month. Surely you have more of an impression than 'great.'"

Shannon chewed her lower lip, watching the desert landscape roll past as she tried to find words for feelings she wasn't sure she understood herself. "He's nothing like what I expected."

"How so?"

"I mean, obviously he looks exactly like Lucas. Identical twins, you know? But the more time I spend with him, the less alike they seem." She paused, remembering the careful way Parker handled the therapy horses, the quiet respect he showed everyone from Dylan to the kids in the program. "Actually, it's weird. Sometimes I look at him and I can barely see the resemblance anymore."

"Interesting. What do you think accounts for the difference?"

Shannon considered the question as she passed a rest area, thinking about the way Parker carried himself. His quiet confidence had nothing to do with charm or manipulation.

"Everything," she said finally. "The way he moves, the way he talks to people, the way he cares about things. Lucas was all surface charm and smooth words. Parker is sincere. Steady. Real."

"Sounds like you've gotten to know him pretty well."

Heat blossomed on Shannon's cheeks as memories from last week surfaced. The office. The table arrangement diagrams. The moment she'd turned to thank him and found his face inches from hers, his gaze dropped to her mouth before snapping back up. The breathless second when she'd wondered if he would lean in.

The terrifying realization that she would have let him.

"Shannon? You still there, honey?"

"Sorry, yes. I was just thinking." Shannon cleared her throat, trying to regain her composure. "He's been incredibly helpful with the gala planning. Patient with all my questions about the ranch facilities, willing to coordinate logistics, and good with the vendors we've met. And all while managing his wrangler duties."

"That's wonderful. It must be a relief to have reliable support."

"It is." Shannon's voice grew quieter. "But Aunt Shirley? I think I might kinda like him. Is that weird?"

The words hung in the air between them, loaded with all the complexity Shannon hadn't been willing to acknowledge until this moment. She'd been attracted to Parker from the beginning—even in her anger and fear that first day, when his voice had stayed calm despite her accusations and his eyes had held concern rather than anger. But somewhere between that first day and now, her attraction had shifted. Deepened. Now when she saw him, her pulse jumped and her thoughts scattered, and she invented reasons to stay in the barn five minutes longer.

"Honey," Aunt Shirley said gently, "have you prayed about it?"

The question caused the muscles in her neck to tense. Had she prayed about Parker? About these growing feelings that left her breathless and confused and hopeful in equal measure?

"I..." Shannon started, then stopped, honesty compelling her toward an admission she wasn't proud of. "No. I haven't."

"Why do you think that is?"

Shannon considered the question as she crested a hill and Wickenburg came into view in the distance. Why hadn't she prayed about him? She prayed about everything else like her work, her future, and her ongoing struggle to fully forgive those who hurt her. Her mother. Lucas.

"I guess I fear what the answer might be," she whispered.

"What are you afraid God might tell you?"

"That I'm being foolish. That after what Lucas did, I should know better than to let someone get this close this quickly. That I'm..." Shannon's throat tightened. "That I'm setting myself up to be hurt again."

"Do you really think Parker is like Lucas?"

"No." The answer came without hesitation, surprising Shannon with its certainty. "No, he's nothing like Lucas. But they have the same appearance, Aunt Shirley. Sometimes I catch myself looking at him, and for just a second, I remember everything Lucas put me through. The lies, the betrayal, the way he made me feel so stupid for trusting him."

"And then what happens?"

Shannon thought about those moments. The flash of

pain when she'd see him from behind and for half a second, her chest would tighten. But then he'd turn, and instead of Lucas's calculating smile, Parker's eyes would crinkle at the corners with genuine warmth. Instead of the slick charm that had once swept her off her feet, there was quiet steadiness that made her shoulders relax.

"Then I remember how Parker has treated me. He's never lied to me, never made me feel foolish for that first day. He's shown me nothing but respect and kindness." Shannon's voice grew stronger. "I know he's not responsible for what his brother did to me."

"That sounds like wisdom to me."

"But is it smart? Getting involved with my ex-boyfriend's identical twin?" Shannon let out a shaky laugh. "It sounds like the setup for a disastrous rom-com movie."

"Or the beginning of something beautiful," Aunt Shirley said. "Shannon, you've spent eight years guarding your heart because of what Lucas did to you. That's understandable, and it was probably necessary for a while. But honey, at some point, healing means being willing to trust again."

Her eyes burned as the truth in her aunt's words settled into her bones. She had been guarding her heart by declining second dates with perfectly nice men, keeping conversations with male colleagues strictly professional, throwing herself into sixty-hour work weeks so there was no room for anything that might crack her careful defenses.

"What if I'm wrong about him?" she whispered. "What if I trust him and he—"

"What if you're right about him?" Aunt Shirley interrupted gently. "What if God has brought someone kind and decent and genuine into your life, and you miss it because you're too afraid to see the gift for what it is?"

The question hung in the air as Shannon turned onto the road leading to Vargas Ranch, the familiar sight of the main buildings coming into view through the mesquite trees. In a few minutes, she'd see Parker again and work alongside him, sharing conversation, laughter, and the growing awareness that had been building between them.

"I think," Shannon said slowly, "I need to start praying about this."

"I think that's a wonderful place to start." Aunt Shirley's voice was warm with approval. "And Shannon? For what it's worth, I have a good feeling about this young man. Sometimes the best things come wrapped in packages we don't expect."

"Thank you," Shannon whispered, pulling into the ranch's parking lot. "For listening. For caring. For always knowing what to say."

"That's what family is for, sweetheart. Now go have a wonderful day with your Parker. And remember, God's plans are often bigger and better than our fears."

As Shannon ended the call and gathered her things from the passenger seat, a gentle peace settled over her. Not the complete resolution of her fears. Those would take time and prayer and continued evidence of Parker's character. But the beginning of hope. The willingness to consider that maybe, just maybe, her heart was ready to trust again.

Walking toward the dining hall, Shannon offered up her first real prayer about the man who was becoming so much more important to her than she'd ever planned to let anyone be.

God, I don't know what I'm doing here. I'm scared and hopeful and confused all at the same time. But if You're opening a door, help me have the courage to walk through it. And if You're not... help me have the wisdom to see that too. Help me see Parker clearly—for who he really is, not through the lens of my past hurt.

It wasn't a perfect prayer, but it was honest.

She tucked her phone into her purse and headed inside, her heart lighter than it had been in weeks.

———

PARKER GRIPPED THE twenty-foot garland strand, his boots planted wide on the dining hall floor as he fed the greenery up to Adan, who balanced on the extended ladder above. The scent of fresh pine filled the space, mixing with the lingering aroma of coffee from Drake's station and the faint smell of horses that seemed to cling to everything at the ranch.

"Little more to the left," Parker called up, eyeing the garland's position against the massive log beam.

Adan adjusted his grip, securing the pine bough.

It had been nearly a month since that first day when Shannon had looked at him with fear and recognition, assuming he was Lucas. He'd been thinking about the journey since then and how her wariness had slowly melted into trust. The woman who'd once called the sheriff on him was becoming the person who understood him better than anyone ever had.

The garland caught on something above, jerking his attention back to the task.

"You're quiet today," Adan observed, securing the pine to a hook on the beam.

"Just concentrating." Which was a lie, and they both knew it.

His thoughts kept circling back to questions he had no business asking. Questions like whether Shannon saw him and not Lucas when she looked at him now. Or if she still caught glimpses of his twin when he moved a certain way or said something that triggered old memories. Questions like whether she felt the same pull toward him he felt toward her.

"Hand me the next section," Adan said, climbing down a few rungs.

Parker moved to the next coil of garland, his boots scuffing against the floor. The dining hall was taking shape for Christmas. The massive tree already stood in its corner, waiting for lights and ornaments, while evergreen swags were slowly transforming the rustic space into something that looked like it belonged in a holiday magazine.

"Parker."

Adan's voice carried a note of amusement that made him look up from the garland he'd been staring at without really seeing.

"You want to tell me what's got you so tangled up you can't focus on simple Christmas decorating?"

Heat crept up Parker's neck. "It's nothing."

"Nothing that's got you looking like someone stole your favorite horse?" Adan climbed down from the ladder, wiping his hands on a rag. "Come on. Talk to me."

He moved to the coffee shop and poured two cups. Parker accepted his, wrapping his hands around the warm ceramic.

"You ever feel as if nothing good can happen to you?" The question came out before he could stop it.

Adan's eyebrows rose slightly. "Every day for about three years after I got hurt. Why?"

Parker stared into his coffee. "Shannon."

"Ah." Adan leaned against the counter. "I wondered when you'd figure that out."

"Figure what out?"

"That you're falling for her." Adan's smile was gentle. "It's been pretty obvious to everyone but you two for weeks."

"She's someone Lucas hurt." The admission scraped Parker's throat raw. "Bad. He stole her college money, destroying her ability to trust. And I look exactly like him."

"And you think she can't tell the difference?"

"I think..." Parker set down his coffee, frustrated by his inability to articulate the fear. "Am I even allowed to feel something for someone my brother hurt?"

Adan was quiet for a moment. "That's not even the right question."

"What do you mean?"

"The question isn't whether you're allowed to love her. It's whether you're brave enough to believe you can be loved back."

Adan was right. Parker wanted to believe Shannon could see past his resemblance to his brother and care for him. Choose him.

"I've spent my whole life cleaning up his messes," Parker said. "Apologizing for things I didn't do. Sometimes I don't even know who I am outside of that."

"Then maybe it's time to find out." Adan moved closer, his voice carrying the authority that had probably helped him face down thousand-pound bulls. "You know what I learned during my riding days? The moment you start riding scared, you're already beaten. Fear makes you tentative, makes you second-guess until you can't trust your own instincts."

"But the opposite's true too. The moment you decide you belong in that arena, that you've earned your place through your skill and courage and the grace of God, everything changes. You stop riding defensively and start riding to win."

"This isn't bull riding, Adan."

"No, it's bigger. It's your life. Your heart." Adan's voice grew more intense. "You think God makes mistakes, Parker? You think He accidentally made you identical twins yet forgot to give you your own purpose?"

The question settled into quiet spaces Parker hadn't examined before. He'd never considered that the God of Christmas Eve services might care about the daily struggles of a ranch hand trying to escape his twin's shadow.

"I don't know," he admitted.

"Well, I do." Adan's certainty was unshakable. "I've watched you work for three months. I've seen how you handle the horses, how you treat people, how you show up every day ready to do what's right even when it's hard. That's not Lucas. That's you. That's who God made you to be."

The weight he'd been carrying shifted, just enough that the tension released from his shoulders.

"And Shannon's a grown woman who makes her own choices," Adan continued. "If she's choosing to spend time with you, to work beside you, to look at you the way I've seen her looking, maybe you should trust her judgment instead of assuming she's too broken to know her own mind."

Parker rubbed a hand behind his neck. "What way?"

"Like you remind her what it feels like to hope again."

The words settled into places that had been cold for longer than he could remember.

"What if I mess it up?" The fear came out raw. "What if I disappoint her?"

"Then you'll apologize and do better. That's what people who care about each other do. They mess up, they make it right, and they keep choosing each other anyway."

Parker went quiet, considering it. Around them, the dining hall waited for completion—garland half-hung, tree standing bare, decorations ready to transform the space for the season and for next week's charity gala. There was work to be done.

But for the first time in months, he felt like he could breathe properly.

"You really think God has a plan for me?"

"Brother, I don't just think it. I know it." Adan clapped a hand on his shoulder. "The question is whether you're ready to stop running from it long enough to see what it looks like."

Parker looked around the dining hall. Three months ago, he'd been just another ranch hand hoping his past wouldn't catch up with him. Now he was part of something meaningful, working alongside people who saw his worth, caring about a woman who made him want to be better than his fears.

"Maybe I am," he said.

"Good." Adan grinned. "Hey, a few of us get together for a Bible study. Nothing fancy—just some guys talking about life, faith, what we're wrestling with. You're welcome anytime."

"I'll think about it."

"Fair enough." Adan grinned and stepped onto the ladder. "Now quit stalling. That garland won't hang itself, and Shannon's going to be here soon."

Parker picked up the next section of garland. For the first time since arriving at Vargas Ranch, he felt like he belonged here not because he was hiding from Lucas's reputation, but because he was building his own.

And if God had a plan for his life—a plan that included Shannon, this work, and a future he'd been afraid to imagine—then maybe it was time to stop fighting it.

Forty minutes later, Parker adjusted the last ornament on the massive tree when the dining hall doors opened. He glanced up, and his hands stilled on the branch.

Shannon stepped inside. She wore a rust sweater that brought out the gold in her eyes. Her gaze found his across the room, and when she smiled, his heart stumbled beneath his ribs.

"This is gorgeous," she breathed, turning slowly to take in the decorations. The massive tree sparkled with lights and ornaments, garland draped every beam in rustic elegance, and the entire space had transformed into a Christmas wonderland that still honored the ranch's character.

Parker wiped his hands on his jeans, suddenly aware of pine sap on his fingers and dust on his shirt. But he didn't look away. He didn't question her attention.

"The florist is going to love this. These pictures will help her create centerpieces that complement what you've already done."

She pulled out her phone, capturing the room from different angles. Parker watched her work, noting the way her eyes brightened as she documented each detail.

"You did good work," she said, smiling at him over her shoulder.

"We make a good team," Parker replied.

Shannon's smile deepened, and in that moment, with Christmas lights reflecting in her eyes and genuine warmth in her expression, he saw what Adan meant.

She wasn't looking at Lucas's ghost. She was looking at him as if he belonged in her story.

He wanted to become the man she thought she saw.

10

Shannon woke before dawn on the morning of the gala, her mind already running through the checklist. As she quickly dressed and drove toward Vargas Ranch, the prayers she'd whispered last night still echoed in her heart. She'd thanked God for bringing Parker into her life and asked for courage to trust what was growing between them.

She arrived just as the first hints of pink touched the eastern sky. As she opened the glass door and stepped into the dining hall, the *clack* of table legs locking into place echoed across the vast room. The scent of freshly brewed coffee hung heavy in the air as Adan shouted over *Rudolph the Red-Nosed Reindeer* blaring from the overhead speakers.

Parker looked up through the controlled chaos when she entered, his smile immediate and genuine. The simple warmth in his eyes soothed the restlessness that had kept her up last night with dreams about red dresses and dancing and finally letting down the walls around her heart.

God had been answering her prayers softly through Parker's character. Through the way he showed up day after day, through moments that revealed his heart. She knew he wasn't his twin. And she was finally learning to trust again.

The first hours were a focused blur. By the time the volunteers arrived at eight, Shannon had already worked with Parker and Adan positioning the heavy auction tables. She marked the exact placement of each dining table with Derin. Then she returned to her laptop at the display table, confirming her timeline: florist at three-thirty, photographer at two. Everything was on schedule.

The transformation continued around her. Chairs had been arranged just so, with black linens draped over tables. She glanced at her watch. Two-fifteen. The photographer should have arrived by now.

That's when her phone rang. The florist.

She pressed her phone to her ear while she stared at the silent auction display table, rethinking the placement of a few items. The florist explained why the centerpieces would be an hour late. Around her, the dining hall buzzed with controlled chaos. Parker's sharp command to Adan cut through the loud, rhythmic tearing of tape as Drake opened boxes of supplies for the dessert station. The faint aroma of chocolate tarts baking, wafted from the kitchen.

"No, I understand that traffic is unpredictable," Shannon said, forcing patience into her voice while mentally recalculating the timeline. "But we have guests arriving at six-thirty, which means everything needs to be perfect by four-thirty."

Shannon ended the call and immediately scrolled to the next crisis on her list. She still needed to finalize the placement of the auction items that had been delivered this morning.

The Phoenix Suns package sat in the bag emblazoned with the team's logo beside her laptop, looking impressive but creating a logistical headache. The courtside Christmas Day tickets, two additional regular season games, signed jerseys, team merchandise, and a basketball autographed by the entire roster. It was easily the crown jewel of tonight's auction, but she second-guessed the presentation.

"Shannon!"

She looked up to see Parker approaching with a steaming cup of her favorite coffee, his sleeves rolled up and dust clinging to his forearms from helping move the heavier tables. The sight of him completely unfazed by the surrounding chaos eased the tension in her shoulders.

"Coffee?" he asked, setting the cup beside her laptop. "Drake says you've been surviving on caffeine fumes since seven this morning."

"I had a granola bar," Shannon protested, though she gratefully wrapped her hands around the warm ceramic. The rich, freshly brewed aroma of the espresso mingled with the sweet scent of vanilla, reminding her that food had been an afterthought today.

"A granola bar is not breakfast on the day you're trying to raise money for kids," Parker said, the gentle reproach in his voice making her stomach flutter in ways that had nothing to do with hunger. "Drake's got fresh muffins. When's the last time you ate something that wasn't wrapped in plastic?"

Shannon opened her mouth to argue, then closed it when she realized she couldn't actually remember yesterday's dinner. "I'll eat after I finish the auction layout."

Parker moved closer, studying the Suns package with the same focused attention he brought to every task around the ranch. "What's the problem?"

"I'm wondering if I should split this up." Shannon gestured toward the collection of basketball memorabilia, her perfectionist tendencies warring with practical concerns. "It's an incredible package, but it's also a huge financial commitment for one bidder. Maybe I'd raise more money by creating multiple lots."

"Hmm." Parker picked up the information sheet, reading through the details. "These Christmas Day tickets are something special. Courtside on Christmas? That's bucket-list territory for any basketball fan."

"Exactly. But if I pair them with everything else, we're talking about a starting bid of at least ten thousand dollars. That eliminates a lot of potential bidders right from the start."

Parker was quiet for a moment, his gaze moving between the tickets and other memorabilia. When he looked at her again, his expression was thoughtful.

"You know what?" He reached out, his shoulder brushing hers as he nudged her gently. "You should make more than one Suns fan happy tonight."

"What do you mean?"

"Keep the Christmas Day tickets as their own auction item. They're so highly coveted, they'll generate serious bidding on their own." Parker's voice carried quiet conviction, like he'd been thinking about this longer than the past five minutes. "Then make the other two regular season games into separate lots. Pair one set with the signed basketball, the other with the team jerseys and merchandise."

Shannon immediately calculated the possibilities. Three separate auction items instead of one massive package. Lower entry points for bidding, which meant more people could take part. More excitement throughout the evening as different groups competed for different prizes.

"That's actually brilliant," she said slowly, as she began mentally restructuring the auction display. "Three separate lots means three distinct moments of peak energy. Three groups of bidders becoming invested."

"And more chances for people to go home happy." Parker's response came quickly, and when Shannon glanced up, he was studying the Christmas Day tickets with an intensity usually reserved for evaluating horses.

His fingers drummed against his thigh. She'd never seen that from him before. Then he caught himself and shoved both hands in his pockets.

"Parker, are you planning to bid tonight?" The question slipped out before she could stop it.

His shoulders tensed. For a heartbeat, he looked like he might deflect entirely. Then he shrugged. "Maybe. If I can afford whatever catches my eye."

But red crept up his neck, spreading to his ears. He wouldn't meet her gaze, suddenly fascinated by the auction materials laid out on the table.

She watched him, reading the nervous energy, the careful avoidance. The way he'd studied those tickets wasn't simple interest. He had been calculating odds. He wanted them. The dream of courtside seats on Christmas Day was clearly a bucket-list item, but she knew exactly what that desire would cost him.

He sent money home to his mom, and the unrecovered lost wages were a constant burden. Betting on tickets like these would mean a significant sacrifice. When she realized he recommended she make it easier for him to bid, her heart swelled with affection. He gave her a perfect strategy, even if it meant giving himself an entry point. If he wished to bet on the tickets, the least she could do was ensure he had the best possible chance.

Finally, Shannon turned back to her laptop, giving him space to recover from his embarrassment.

"Three separate lots it is," she said, opening a new document to revise the auction listings. "You're right. This will work much better."

Parker smiled, clearly pleased. "Good. Now about that muffin..."

Before she could object, he made a beeline for the coffee counter and came back with a blueberry muffin that smelled of brown sugar and melted butter. It was a testament to a baker who took joy in feeding people well.

"Eat," Parker said, placing it beside her coffee with a gentle authority that suggested he wasn't taking no for an answer. "Your brain needs fuel if you're going to pull off the event of the decade."

Shannon took a bite. Hunger she hadn't noticed suddenly roared to life. The muffin tasted perfect. Sweet but not overwhelming with bursts of tart blueberry that reminded her exactly how much she'd been neglecting herself in the rush to make everything perfect.

"Better?" Parker asked, settling into the chair beside her as she continued eating.

"Much better," Shannon admitted. "Thank you. For the food, for the auction advice, for..." She gestured around the dining hall. "For all of this."

The Christmas tree stood in its corner, now fully decorated with lights that would create magic once the sun went down. Garland draped every beam, creating rustic elegance that complemented rather than competed with the holiday decorations. The tables were draped in black linens that would showcase the white rose centerpieces perfectly, and the entire space hummed with the energy of something special about to happen.

"We make a good team," Parker said quietly, his gaze holding hers.

Something fluttered low in her stomach, light and unsettling in the best way. They did make a good team. More than that, they fit together in ways she hadn't expected, complementing each other's strengths and covering each other's weaknesses.

"Yeah." The word came out barely above a whisper. "We do."

The air between them seemed to still, like the entire world paused, letting this moment settle.

A crash from the kitchen area shattered it. Drake's voice called out that everything was fine, just a dropped tray. Shannon's phone buzzed against the table with another vendor update, and just like that, the moment dissolved.

But as she answered the call and Parker joined Adan to arrange the last few tables, Shannon stole glances at him throughout the conversation. The way he moved with quiet efficiency, never getting in anyone's way but always exactly where he was needed. The patience he showed when Dylan's stutter made directions unclear. The gentle smile he offered Adan when his friend looked overwhelmed by the scope of what they were attempting.

This was the man Lucas had never been — steady, thoughtful, and genuine in his care for others.

And Shannon saw it now. Not just with her eyes, but with something deeper. A quiet knowing. A stirring in her heart.

Maybe Aunt Shirley was right. Maybe the prayers she'd whispered in the dark — about opening her heart, about letting those walls fall and trusting God with her fears — were finally being answered. Not in a rush. Not in some dramatic revelation. But in the steady presence of a man who showed up. Who listened. Who led with kindness.

She hadn't expected Parker. Hadn't expected the way his constancy would chip away at her doubt. The way his character would speak louder than any promise.

Slowly, she was changing. Not because she'd decided to, but because grace had found her in the quiet moments. In the way Parker looked at her like she mattered. In the way he never pushed, never performed — just lived with integrity.

He probably wouldn't betray her. His character remained constant. And maybe she could trust that.

By late afternoon, the dining hall transformation was complete. Auction tables displayed items ranging from luxury vacation packages to handcrafted artwork to Parker's newly separated Phoenix Suns lots. The dining tables stood ready, awaiting only the centerpieces. The greenery on the beams filled the room with a subtle pine scent. Even the amber lighting created the warm, welcoming atmosphere Shannon had envisioned.

"This is incredible," Braden's mother, Brisa, said, emerging from the kitchen where she'd been helping with the catering team. "I can't believe this is the same room where we eat lunch every day."

Shannon felt a swell of pride as she looked around the space. It was incredible — professional enough to impress Phoenix's wealthy elite, but warm enough to feel personal and meaningful. The perfect setting for launching Braden's Hope into its next phase.

"It's going to be a magical evening," she said, meaning every word.

Parker appeared at her elbow, close enough that she caught the scent of his soap mixed with the honest smell of work. "Speaking of magical," he said quietly, "you should probably go get ready. Guests start arriving in two hours, and you've earned the chance to enjoy your own party."

The reminder sent a flutter of nervous excitement through Shannon's stomach. In two hours, everything she'd worked toward for the past month would finally happen. Success or failure, triumph or disaster—it would all be determined by how well she'd planned and how generously people responded to the cause she'd grown to love.

"What if something goes wrong?" The fear slipped out before she could stop it, raw and honest in a way that surprised them both.

Parker turned to face her fully, his hands settling on her shoulders with firm, supportive weight. "Then we'll figure it out," he said, his voice carrying absolute certainty. "Together. That's what we do."

The simple words settled into Shannon's chest like an anchor, steadying her against the waves of pre-event anxiety that had been building all day. He was right. They would figure it out. Whatever happened tonight, she wouldn't be facing it alone.

"Together," she repeated, testing the word and finding it felt exactly right.

Parker smiled, his hands squeezing her shoulders briefly before he stepped back. "Now go get beautiful. Not that you need any help with that."

The compliment, delivered with sincerity rather than smooth charm, sent warmth flooding through Shannon's cheeks. As she gathered her things and headed toward her car, she looked forward to the evening with anticipation rather than anxiety.

Tonight would be special. She could feel it in her bones. And when Parker saw her in the red dress she'd chosen specifically for this moment, when they danced together, maybe she'd finally have the courage to tell him how she really felt.

Maybe tonight would be the beginning of something even more beautiful than the successful charity gala she'd worked so hard to create.

For the first time in years, Shannon was ready to bet her heart on the possibility of love.

———

PARKER GRIPPED ONE end of the heavy stage section while Adan took the other, their boots scuffing against the dining hall's wood floor as they maneuvered it into position. The sun streamed through the windows, illuminating dust motes that danced in the air disturbed by all the activity.

"Little more to the left," Adan directed, adjusting his grip.

Parker shifted his weight, muscles straining as they settled the platform into place. Around them, the dining hall buzzed with purposeful chaos. Devon worked behind them, already pulling out coils of cable for the sound system. Derin and a couple of other ranch hands carried in stacks of cushioned chairs, their fabric covers a neutral beige that would complement the evergreen and gold theme Shannon had chosen. Across the room, Brisa and Solana moved between tables with crisp black tablecloths, their conversation a pleasant backdrop to the work. The espresso machine's constant whir sounded as resort guests braved the chaos for their favorite caffeine fix.

And somewhere in all this controlled mayhem was Shannon, her laptop at the ready and her phone pressed to her ear as she coordinated the thousand details that would transform this space into something magical by evening.

Parker straightened, rolling his shoulders to ease the tension. A week had passed since his conversation with Adan about Shannon, and about God maybe having a plan for his life that had nothing to do with Lucas. He'd attended one early morning Bible study Adan had invited him to—awkward at first, sitting among men who spoke about faith with the same casual certainty they discussed horse training or weather patterns. But something about the quiet morning had settled into Parker's bones, making him wonder if maybe there was something to this God business after all.

"Speakers next?" Adan asked, pulling Parker from his thoughts.

"Yeah."

They moved to where the sound equipment waited, boxed and ready for setup. Parker lifted one of the speaker stands while Adan grabbed the other, and they carried them toward opposite sides of the stage.

"You nervous about tonight?" Adan's question came casually, but Parker caught the knowing look in his friend's eyes.

"Some." Parker positioned the stand, checking that it was level. "Shannon's put everything into this. I just want it to go well for her."

"It will." Adan's confidence was absolute. "The woman's been planning this down to the minute. I've never seen someone so organized."

Parker smiled despite himself, thinking about the color-coded spreadsheets Shannon had shown him, the backup plans for the backup plans, the way she'd triple-checked every detail until he'd gently suggested she might be overthinking it. She'd laughed then, admitted he was probably right, and then gone back to checking her lists, anyway.

"She's something," Parker said.

"That she is." Adan glanced at him, amusement flickering across his features. "You planning on telling her that?"

Heat crept up Parker's neck. "Maybe. Eventually."

"Eventually, huh?" Adan's grin widened. "Brother, you've got the patience of a saint."

Before Parker could respond, one of the Vargas brothers—Devon, he thought—appeared beside them with an armload of cables. "You guys done with the stage? I need to run the sound lines."

"All yours," Adan confirmed, stepping back.

They moved to the stacks of chairs waiting along the wall. Parker grabbed one in each hand. Shannon had fought for these chairs, he remembered, insisting that folding metal wouldn't convey the right message for a fundraiser trying to attract serious donors. Seeing her vision come to life, he fully understood it now.

"Eight to a table," Parker said, more to himself than Adan as they began arranging chairs around the first table Brisa had finished covering.

They fell into a rhythm—carry, position, adjust, repeat. The work was mindless enough that Parker's thoughts drifted to tonight, to how the room would look filled with guests in their fancy dresses and suits, to the auction Shannon had organized, to the speeches that would tell the stories of kids whose lives had been changed by Braden's Hope.

To Shannon herself, moving through it all with that quiet competence he admired.

"You got something to wear tonight?" Adan's question broke into Parker's thoughts as they positioned chairs around the third table.

Parker hesitated, the question hitting closer to the nervousness that had been building all morning. "Jeans and a button-down shirt. My boots are polished."

"But?"

"But nothing. That's what I've got." Parker set down the chair harder than necessary, frustration bleeding through. "It's a charity gala, Adan. Everyone's going to be in suits and ties, and I'm going to look like the ranch hand I am."

Adan paused, studying him with a steady gaze that

missed nothing. "You are a ranch hand. Nothing wrong with that."

"I know. But..." Parker struggled to articulate the feeling that had been gnawing at him since he'd seen the first RSVP confirmations from Phoenix's wealthy donors. "Shannon's worked so hard on this. She's brought in people with money and influence. And I'm going to be the guy who shows up looking like he just came from mucking stalls."

"First of all, you're not mucking stalls tonight. Second, nobody's going to care what you're wearing." Adan's voice carried the calm certainty of someone who'd faced down bigger fears than dress codes. "You're here because you helped make this happen. You earned your place at this event just like anyone else."

The words echoed what Adan had said last week about earning his place, about belonging in the arena. Parker wanted to believe it. But the old insecurities ran deep, carved by years of being judged, of not measuring up, of paying for sins that weren't his.

"You really think so?"

"I know so." Adan grabbed two more chairs, nodding for Parker to do the same. "Besides, do you think Shannon cares whether you're wearing a sports coat? That woman sees who you are, Parker. She's not looking at your clothes."

He thought about that as they continued setting up chairs. About how Shannon had looked at him this past week, the growing ease between them, the way she'd started seeking him out not just for work but for conversation, for company, for the simple pleasure of being around each other.

Maybe Adan was right. Maybe his appearance didn't matter as much as his presence.

"You'll be fine," Adan said, clapping him on the shoulder as they finished the fourth table. "Trust me on this."

Parker nodded, wanting to believe it even as doubt still whispered in the back of his mind.

They worked steadily for the next hour, the dining hall gradually transforming around them. The stage stood ready for the event. Chairs surrounded tables covered with black cloths. Devon had the sound system wired and was running tests. Derin directed the placement of the last few tables, his foreman's eye ensuring proper spacing for guests to move comfortably through the room.

And through it all, Shannon moved like a conductor orchestrating a symphony—checking details, answering questions, and solving problems before they became crises. Parker watched her when he thought she wouldn't notice, amazed by her composure, by the way she made everything look effortless even though he knew she'd been running on determination and coffee for days.

"Centerpieces are running late," she announced to the room at large, her phone still pressed to her ear. "But they'll be here by four-thirty. We're fine."

The slight edge in her voice suggested she wasn't entirely convinced they were fine, but nobody challenged her. They'd all learned that Shannon had contingency plans for her contingency plans.

"Looking good," Dylan called from the stage. "We'll be ready."

Shannon's shoulders relaxed fractionally, and she offered him a grateful smile before diving back into her phone conversation with whoever was handling the floral arrangements.

By midafternoon, the setup was complete except for the missing centerpieces and the final sound check. Parker stood near the entrance, taking in the transformed space. It was elegant without being stuffy, festive without being over the top.

"Alright, people," Dylan announced. "We've got a few hours until the guests arrive. Everyone go get cleaned up. Thanks again for your help."

The group began dispersing, tired but satisfied with

their work. Parker caught Shannon's eye across the room, and she gave him a quick smile—grateful, warm, a little frazzled—before turning back to her laptop.

He wanted to go to her, to tell her how incredible this was, how proud he was of everything she'd accomplished. But she was still in work mode, still coordinating and planning, and he didn't want to distract her from what she needed to do.

Tonight. He'd find the right moment tonight.

Parker headed out to his truck. The afternoon was still pleasantly warm. The drive to the bunkhouse took only minutes, and he used the time to think about the evening ahead. About seeing Shannon in whatever she'd chosen to wear—he'd overheard her mention something about a dress to Brisa last week, but she'd been vague on details. About watching her see the culmination of all her work as guests filled that beautiful space and opened their wallets for the cause she cared about so deeply. They both did.

About maybe, possibly, finding the courage to tell her about his growing feelings.

The bunkhouse was quiet when Parker arrived, most of the other hands still finishing afternoon chores or already in town for their evening off. He grabbed his towel and headed for the showers, letting hot water work the tension from his muscles and wash away the dust and sweat of the day's work.

Back at his bunk, he pulled out his nicest pair of jeans—dark wash, no fraying, the ones he saved for town trips and church services. He'd polished his nicest boots to a shine last night. And the white button-down shirt he'd picked up at a thrift store in Wickenburg hung pressed and ready on his closet door.

It was the best he had. It would have to be enough.

Parker dressed carefully, taking his time with the shirt buttons, making sure everything sat right. He checked his reflection in the small mirror above his the bathroom sink, hardly recognizing the man staring back at him. Clean-shaven. Hair combed. A dust-free cowboy hat. Clothes that looked almost nice enough for the occasion.

Almost.

A sports coat would help. Would make him look like he belonged among the donors and guests who'd paid good money to attend this event. Would make him feel less like an imposter and more like someone Shannon could be proud to have beside her.

But he didn't have one, and wishing wouldn't change that.

Parker adjusted his collar one more time, then forced himself to step back from the mirror. Adan's words echoed in his mind. *Nobody's going to care what you're wearing. You earned your place at this event.*

He wanted to believe that. Wanted to walk into that dining hall with his head high, confident in who he was rather than worried about what he lacked.

The sun was starting its descent toward the horizon, painting the sky in shades of orange and gold. In a few hours, guests would begin arriving. The gala Shannon had poured her heart into would finally happen. And Parker would be there, supporting her in the best way he knew how.

Even if he looked like a ranch hand trying to play dress-up.

He grabbed his keys and headed back out to his truck, anticipation and nervousness warring in his gut. Whatever tonight brought, whatever happened between him and Shannon, at least he'd be there. At least he'd stopped running from the possibility of something good long enough to see what it might become.

The drive back to the main ranch buildings felt different this time, weighted with possibility. Parker's thoughts drifted to Shannon's dedication, to the kids the fundraiser would help, to the woman who'd made it all happen through sheer determination and heart.

He was so proud of her. Proud of what she'd built and proud of how she'd fought for this program.

Tonight, he'd tell her that. Somehow, someway, he'd find the words to let her know how much she meant to him.

And maybe if he was lucky, she'd let him be a part of whatever came next.

Parker pulled into the parking lot near the dining hall just as the florist's van arrived with the centerpieces. Perfect timing. He could help unload, make himself useful, and maybe glimpse Shannon before the evening officially began.

Before he had to figure out how to look confident in a room full of people who'd never know what it meant to him just to be there.

One thing at a time. Help with the centerpieces. Support Shannon. Make it through this evening without embarrassing himself or her.

And try not to think too hard about the sports coat he didn't have and the insecurities that wouldn't quite stay quiet no matter how much he wanted them to.

11

SHANNON STOOD AT the edge of the dining hall, her red evening gown flowing around her like liquid silk, and her breath hitched at the transformation before her. The space that had been chaos just this morning now gleamed with polished refinement—round tables draped in black linens, centerpieces of white roses and desert sage creating rustic charm, the massive Christmas tree sparkling with lights and crowned by that beautiful antique star. Soft Christmas carols played overhead.

They had folded back the glass-paneled, opening to the patio where string lights created a canopy of stars overhead and heaters waited to ward off the December chill. Silent auction tables lined the walls, displaying everything from the Phoenix Suns courtside tickets to high-end smart home systems, from luxury spa packages to the custom artwork she'd watched local artisans create specifically for tonight.

Two hundred and fifteen confirmed guests, with walk-ins likely to push that number even higher. She'd done it. Actually done it.

"Shannon."

She turned to find Dylan approaching, looking sharp in a dark suit but carrying himself with the tension of someone facing a firing squad rather than a friendly crowd. Nervousness had replaced his quiet confidence, and her heart went out to him.

"You look terrified," she said, smoothing an imaginary wrinkle from his tie. "But you shouldn't be. You've got this."

"I d-d-don't know about that," Dylan replied, his stutter more pronounced than usual. "There are a l-l-lot of people here."

"There are many people here because they believe in what you and Adan are building," Shannon corrected. "They want to support Braden's Hope, and that's because of the foundation you've laid with the equine therapy program."

She glanced toward the front of the room where Brisa offered him an encouraging smile. "Besides, you've practiced this speech a dozen times with Brisa, and she'll be right there in the front row. Just look at her if you get nervous."

Dylan's expression softened at the mention of his girlfriend. "She's been p-p-patient with me."

"She loves you," Shannon said. "And everyone in this room respects what you're doing. You're not performing for strangers. You're sharing your heart with people who are already on your side."

"Thank you," Dylan whispered. "For all of this. I know it w-w-wasn't easy to pull together so quickly."

She absorbed the praise with quiet satisfaction before her focus moved to the entrance. Guests were arriving in earnest now. She recognized several prominent Phoenix business leaders, local politicians, and at least three people she was certain would bid aggressively on the high-end auction items.

"I need to check a few things," she told Dylan. "But you're going to be wonderful up there. Trust me."

She wove through the rows of tables, catching details that others might miss. The auction screens were displayed prominently. The beverage stations were staffed and ready. The catering team from the resort kitchen circulated with appetizers that looked as elegant as they tasted.

From his dessert station, Drake flashed her a grin that radiated pure excitement about the evening ahead.

Everything was flawless. Everything was ready.

So why did she feel like she was forgetting something crucial?

Shannon pulled out her phone to check her notes for the hundredth time, scanning through the timeline she'd memorized: cocktail hour until seven-thirty, welcome remarks from Dylan and Adan at eight, dinner service while guests browsed the silent auction, followed by dancing until whenever people called it a night.

"You look like someone who's about to conquer the world."

The familiar voice snagged her attention. Parker approached, and electric waves radiated down her spine.

He looked incredible. Dark jeans that fit him perfectly, a crisp white button-down shirt, and a navy sport coat that emphasized the breadth of his shoulders and brought out the blue of his eyes. Someone—probably Adan, given the cut and quality—had helped him dress for the occasion, and the result was devastating to her carefully maintained composure.

"You clean up pretty well yourself," Shannon managed, hoping her voice sounded steadier than she felt.

Something flickered in Parker's expression as his gaze traveled over her red gown, lingering for just a moment before meeting her eyes again. "You look..." He paused, seeming to search for words. "Beautiful doesn't seem like enough."

Heat spread on her cheeks at the sincerity in his voice, at the way he was looking at her like he'd never quite seen her before. The red gown had been an impulsive purchase, more elegant and eye-catching than anything she usually wore to professional events. But seeing Parker's reaction made every penny worth it.

"Thank you," she breathed. "For everything. I couldn't

have pulled this off without your help these past few weeks."

"You could have," Parker replied with quiet conviction. "You're remarkable at this. But I'm glad I got to be part of it."

The moment stretched between them, loaded with things she wasn't quite ready to say, until the sound of laughter from a nearby table reminded Shannon that they were standing in the middle of a room full of people who expected her to be the gracious hostess.

"I should—" she began.

"Go," Parker said with a smile. "I'll be around if you need anything."

Shannon greeted donors and guests as she navigated the crowd with renewed energy, ensuring everyone felt welcomed and appreciated. Photographers captured candid moments of guests examining auction items. Wealthy business owners greeted each other with hearty handshakes. Several of the Suns players' wives generated excitement around the courtside tickets.

Everything was working exactly as she'd planned.

"Shannon!"

She turned to see Braden's mother, Brisa, approaching with a smile that lit up her entire face. The young woman looked radiant in her navy dress, her long blond hair styled in a graceful updo. She looked both sophisticated and approachable.

"Brisa, you look absolutely lovely," Shannon said, pulling the other woman into a quick hug. "How's our star speaker doing?"

"Nervous but ready," Brisa replied with a laugh. "Dylan's been practicing his speech all week, but I think he's more worried about stuttering in front of this crowd than about forgetting what to say."

"He'll be ideal," Shannon assured her. "The message matters more than perfect delivery, and no one cares more about these kids than Dylan does."

"That's what I keep telling him." Brisa's expression grew more serious. "I can't thank you enough for making this happen. What you're doing for Braden, for all the children who'll benefit from this program, means everything to our family."

Shannon's throat tightened at the gratitude in Brisa's voice. This was why she did this work, why the long hours and endless details were worth it. Somewhere in this room full of evening wear and expensive food was a little boy who would have access to life-changing therapy because people had cared.

"Braden's the one doing the hard work," Shannon replied. "We're just making sure he can keep growing stronger."

A commotion near the entrance caught her attention, and Shannon looked over to see Aunt Shirley arriving in grand style. At seventy-two, her great-aunt still commanded attention wherever she went, tonight wearing a midnight blue gown that complemented her silver hair and carrying herself with the poise that had served her well during decades of working with Hollywood's elite.

"Excuse me," Shannon told Brisa. "I need to go greet the woman who taught me everything I know about putting on a show."

She made her way through the crowd toward Aunt Shirley, noting with satisfaction how many people turned to watch the elegant older woman's entrance. If Shannon had inherited anything from her great-aunt beyond a work ethic, it was an appreciation for the importance of making moments feel special.

"Aunt Shirley," she said, reaching her great-aunt and accepting the warm hug that always felt like coming home. "You look absolutely regal."

"As do you, my dear. That red dress is perfect—sophisticated, but with just enough drama to make a certain cowboy remember you." Aunt Shirley's eyes sparkled with approval as she took in the transformed dining hall. "And this? This is magnificent. You've outdone yourself."

"I had a good teacher," Shannon replied, meaning it. "Thank you for coming."

"Are you kidding? Miss my great-niece's triumphant debut leading a new charity? I wouldn't dream of it." Aunt Shirley's gaze sharpened as it moved around the room. "Besides, I'm curious to see what kind of bidding war develops over those basketball tickets."

Something in her aunt's tone made Shannon look at her more closely. "You're not thinking of bidding, are you? "

"Oh, I might," Aunt Shirley replied with a mysterious smile. "I am very interested in supporting young love when I see it."

Before Shannon could ask what that meant, the sound of silverware against glass drew everyone's attention toward the front of the room. Dylan stood behind the microphone, looking pale but determined, with Adan beside him radiating a confidence that came from years in the spotlight as a pro bull rider.

"Ladies and gentlemen," Adan said, his voice carrying easily through the room, "if we could have your attention, we'd like to share a few words about why you're all here tonight."

The crowd settled into expectant silence, and Shannon's pulse quickened with anticipation. This was when all her planning would be put to the test, when the success or failure of the evening would be determined by how well they'd prepared.

Dylan stepped forward to the microphone, his gaze finding Brisa in the front row exactly as Shannon had suggested. When he spoke, his voice was quiet but steady, the stutter barely noticeable as he focused on the woman he loved and the cause that mattered to both of them.

"Three months ago," Dylan began, "a little boy named

Braden taught me something about courage."

Tears pricked Shannon's eyes as Dylan's nervousness transformed into genuine passion, his love for the children they served shining through every carefully chosen word. This was why she'd believed in this project from the beginning. Not because of the money they'd raise or the attention they'd generate, but because of moments like this when people opened their hearts to something bigger than themselves.

As Dylan finished his remarks and handed the microphone to Adan, Shannon caught Parker's eye across the room. He was watching her with an expression she couldn't quite read, something intense and determined that made her pulse skip.

Tonight was going to be more than just a successful fundraiser, she realized. Tonight was going to change everything.

———

PARKER STOOD AT the back of the crowd, his hands shoved deep in his pockets as he listened to Adan work the room with a natural charisma that had probably served him well during his bull riding days. Dylan had done great with his speech—better than great, actually—but now it was Adan's turn to charm the wealthy donors into opening their wallets.

"What you've seen tonight," Adan was saying, his voice carrying easily through the dining hall, "results from one woman's vision and determination. Shannon Burke didn't just organize this event. She created a bridge between our community and the children who need our help the most."

Applause rippled through the crowd, and Parker found his gaze drawn inevitably toward Shannon, standing near the front with that radiant smile that made his chest tight. The red dress moved like liquid fire in the soft lighting, and every time she turned or gestured, he caught another glimpse of elegant lines that made him forget how to breathe properly.

When she'd walked into the dining hall earlier, he'd actually stopped mid-conversation with one of the ranch hands. Just stopped, words dying in his throat, because Shannon Burke in a red evening gown was something his brain apparently couldn't process while also managing basic functions like speech.

That's when Adan had appeared at his elbow with a navy sport coat draped over his arm.

"Brought this from the bunkhouse," Adan had said, offering it without fanfare. "Thought you might want to look the part tonight."

Parker could hardly believe that on a night when Adan had every reason to focus elsewhere, he'd still carved out time to think about Parker's comfort—to help him feel like he belonged. That's what real friends did. And it's what Parker had been longing for since the day he arrived at Vargas Ranch. Maybe longer.

"Now," Adan continued, "we'll move into our silent auction, where you'll find items generously donated by businesses and individuals who believe in second chances and new beginnings. Just scan the QR code to get the app where you can place your bids. Before I try to outbid you all for those Suns tickets, I want to personally thank the man who's been the silent backbone of our equine therapy program."

Parker's attention snapped back to the front of the room as Adan's gaze found his across the crowd.

"Parker Quaid has been with us for just three months, but in that time, he's become essential to everything we do. He's the one who makes sure our therapy horses are ready for sessions like Braden's. He's the one who stays late to ensure every detail is perfect. And he believes in these kids as much as anyone in this room."

Heat crept up Parker's neck as the crowd turned to look at him, applause building despite his desire to disappear into the floor. He managed a nod of acknowledgment, but his throat felt too tight for words.

He wasn't used to being recognized for anything positive. Ever. He wasn't used to having his name mentioned in front of two hundred people without it being followed by accusations or suspicion. His throat clogged.

"Thank you, Parker." The grin on Adan's face told him this discomfort was intentional and necessary. Adan would not let him hide anymore. "Now, let's raise some money for these kids."

As the crowd dispersed toward the silent auction tables, Parker made his way toward a high-top table on the patio, needing a moment to collect himself. The evening was exceeding expectations. He could see it in the animated conversations as people examined the auction items, in the way donors pulled out their phones to scan QR codes, and in the energy that buzzed through the room like electricity.

"You look like you need this."

Parker turned to find Dylan approaching with two glasses of what looked like soda, his earlier nervousness gone.

"Thanks," Parker said, accepting the glass gratefully. "You did good up there."

"Thanks to Shannon. And Brisa." Dylan's expression softened as he glanced toward where his girlfriend chatted with a group of potential donors. "She m-m-made me practice until I could say it without thinking about the words."

"Smart woman."

"The smartest." Dylan took a sip of his soda, then looked at Parker with amusement. "Speaking of smart women, you planning to bid on anything tonight?"

The question was casual, but Parker detected the undercurrent in Dylan's tone. Of course, Dylan had noticed him staring at the Suns tickets during their setup earlier. The man missed little.

"Maybe," Parker said carefully.

"Those basketball tickets are going to sell for serious money," Dylan observed. "Christmas Day, courtside seats? Could be fifteen, twenty thousand or more."

Parker's stomach clenched at the numbers, even though he'd been calculating the same figures all week. His savings account—what was left after legal complications caused by his twin and the move to central Arizona—contained exactly four thousand, three hundred and twenty-seven dollars. Not nearly enough to win a bidding war against Phoenix's wealthy elite.

But he had to try.

Shannon had looked at those tickets with longing usually reserved for impossible dreams. Because she'd given up her season tickets to pay for college after Lucas destroyed her financial security. Because she'd spent weeks working sixteen-hour days to make tonight possible, and she deserved to have something wonderful for herself.

Somewhere over the past month, watching her work, listening to her laugh, and seeing the way she treated everyone from billionaire donors to four-year-old clients with the same genuine care, he'd fallen hard for her, despite all the reasons he shouldn't.

"Excuse me," Parker said, setting down his glass. "I need to go look at something."

The auction table displayed an iPad showing the current bid status of all the silent auction items. Parker worked his way through the crowd until he could see the screen, his heart sinking as he scanned the numbers displayed there.

The opening bid for the Christmas Day tickets had been two thousand dollars. In the fifteen minutes since the auction opened, it had climbed to three thousand, with the app showing six different bidders had participated. At the top of the screen, the current high bid showed four thousand dollars.

Parker stared at the number, calculating rapidly. Even if he emptied his savings account entirely, he doubted he could win. But maybe if he bid what he had, it would at least drive the price higher. Maybe Shannon would see that he'd tried, that he'd wanted to give her something special.

He pulled out his phone and accessed the auction app, entering his bidder number and his entire savings.

The number looked pathetic compared to the others, but it represented everything he had. Every dollar he'd managed to save over the years, every bit of financial security he'd built.

"That's a generous bid."

Parker turned to find an older woman beside him, dressed in a dark blue gown. Her short, spiky silver hair and kind eyes seemed to see everything. She looked familiar, but he couldn't quite place where he'd seen her before.

"Not generous enough," he admitted, stepping back from the table to make room for other bidders.

"Oh, I don't know about that," the woman said with a smile that held secrets. "Sometimes the gesture matters more than the amount."

Before Parker could ask what she meant, the iPad screen refreshed with a new high bid. Parker watched his own number disappear as the total climbed to ten thousand, then fifteen, to twenty-two.

He'd known this would happen. Had known from the moment he decided to bid that he couldn't compete with the money in this room. But disappointment hung around his shoulders like a heavy winter coat. He had wanted so badly to do this one thing for her.

"Parker!"

He turned as Shannon crossed the dining hall, her heels tapping against the wood floor, her smile radiant.

"The final totals just came in," she said, breathless. "Five hundred thousand dollars. I didn't think we'd even break half of that."

"That's incredible," Parker said, meaning it despite the quiet sting behind his ribs. "You should be proud. You made this happen."

"We made it happen," she said, then threw her arms around him, laughter spilling against his shoulder. "We can fund the whole expansion. Equine therapist, horses, gear. Everything we planned."

He held her close, her joy vibrating through him like a struck chord. The scent of warm cinnamon and vanilla clung to her hair, and he pressed his cheek to her temple, savoring the moment.

"You did it," he whispered. "You made it real."

She stepped back, eyes damp, gaze steady. The look she gave him hit harder than applause or numbers ever could.

"Dance with me," she said. "Please. I want to celebrate with you."

The DJ played a slow tune. Couples drifted onto the dance floor, framed by the silhouettes of mesquite trees and under a canopy of string lights and stars.

Parker hesitated. He didn't dance. And standing so close to Shannon, with her looking at him like that, felt like stepping into dangerous territory.

But when she reached for his hand, leading him toward the dance floor, he didn't flinch.

She settled one hand on his shoulder, the other in his, and he placed his hand at the small of her back. The crowd nudged them together. Her body fit against his like a rhythm he'd known without realizing. They moved in time with the music, her breath brushing his neck.

"Thank you," she murmured. "For everything you did to make tonight happen."

"Thank you for letting me be a part of it," he said, his hand steady at the small of her back, anchoring her close.

They swayed, moving as one, wrapped in the warmth of shared victory. The waltz carried other couples past, but Parker focused only on Shannon. The way she leaned into him, the hush of her breathing, the trust in every step.

"Parker." Her fingers tensed slightly on his shoulder, and he drew back enough to see her expression.

"Yeah?"

"Why did you bid on the basketball tickets?"

The question hit him like cold water, and he tensed despite his efforts to stay relaxed. "What makes you think I bid on them?"

"I saw your bid on the app earlier. Four thousand three hundred dollars." Shannon's eyes searched his face. "That's not a small amount of money for someone just starting over."

Parker's throat tightened. Of course, she'd noticed. Shannon noticed everything, especially when it came to important details.

"It wasn't enough anyway," he said, trying for casual and missing by miles.

"That's not what I asked." Shannon stopped dancing, her hands still on his shoulders but her expression serious. "Why did you bid everything you had on those tickets?"

The question hung between them. Loaded with implications Parker wasn't sure he was ready to face. Around them, other couples continued dancing, oblivious to the moment of truth unfolding in their midst.

He could deflect. Could make up something about supporting the charity or getting caught up in auction fever. Could protect himself the way he'd been protecting himself for years.

But this was Shannon. The woman who'd apologized sincerely for misjudging him, who'd listened without judgment as he'd shared his deepest family wounds, who'd seen him at his most vulnerable and hadn't turned away.

"Because you said it would be amazing to go to the Christmas Day game," he said. "Because you gave up your season tickets to pay for college after Lucas took your money. Because you deserved to have something wonderful after all the work you put into making tonight happen."

Shannon stared at him, something shifting in her expression that made his heart race with equal parts hope and terror.

"You bid your entire savings account," she whispered, "to give me something I wanted."

"Yeah," Parker said. "I did."

The admission hung in the air between them, more honest than anything he'd shared before. On the stage, the DJ transitioned to another slow song, but Parker barely heard it over the sound of his own heart pounding in his ears.

"That's the most romantic and selfless thing anyone's ever done for me." Her voice broke on the last word.

Before Parker could respond, before he could process what her words meant, Shannon rose on her toes and kissed him.

The world narrowed to the warmth of her lips against his, soft and tentative, asking a question he'd been afraid to answer. His arms tightened around her waist, pulling her closer as he kissed her back—no longer a question but an answer, a promise, recognition of everything that had been building between them since the day after they met.

When they finally broke apart, he couldn't look away. Her eyes held his, breathless and wondering. For a moment, neither of them moved.

Until a wry smile crossed her face.

"You'll never believe this."

"What?"

Shannon nodded toward the woman in blue. "That's Aunt Shirley. And she just asked me if I knew someone who might like to take her great-niece to a basketball game."

Parker stared at her, the words not quite computing through the haze of everything that had just happened—the kiss as an admission of his feelings, the overwhelming success of the evening.

"She... what?" His voice came out rough, disbelieving.

"Twenty-two thousand dollars for courtside seats to the Christmas Day game," Shannon said softly, her eyes bright with tears and something that looked like wonder. "And she wants you to take me."

The full impact hit him then, stealing his breath completely. Aunt Shirley—Shannon's great-aunt, Dylan's speech pathologist, the woman who'd somehow seen right through his pathetic bid to the heart of what he'd been trying to do—had spent a fortune to give them something he'd only dreamed of providing.

"Parker?" Shannon's voice was gentle, concerned. "Are you okay?"

He wasn't okay. He was overwhelmed, grateful beyond words, and terrified that he'd wake up and discover this whole evening had been some impossible dream.

"She did that for us?" he managed.

"She did that for you," Shannon corrected. "Because she saw what you would give up for me, and she wanted to make sure you didn't have to."

His throat closed. In thirty years of life, no one—outside of his parents—had ever made a gesture like this for him. No one had seen him struggling and stepped in to help, not expecting anything in return, just because they thought he was a good man.

"I don't know what to say," he whispered.

"Say you'll take me to the game," Shannon replied, her smile soft and hopeful. "Say you'll let me cheer too loudly and probably spill nachos on your shirt."

Parker laughed.

"Shannon Burke," he said, his hands framing her face, his thumbs brushing away the tears of joy on her cheeks, "would you go to the Phoenix Suns Christmas Day game with me?"

"Yes." Her hand slid to the back of his neck as she kissed him again, softer this time, a promise sealed. "Yes, I would love to."

Around them, the gala continued with couples dancing, donors celebrating, and the sound of laughter and conversation filling the transformed dining hall. But in that moment, Parker was aware only of Shannon in his arms, of the precious gift they'd been given, and of the way the future suddenly looked brighter than he'd ever dared imagine.

He just hoped—maybe even prayed—it wasn't a mirage.

12

SHANNON PRESSED HER back against the wooden fence rail, watching Parker lead Miracle through her cool-down routine in the crisp December morning air. The mare's breath created small puffs of vapor in the forty-degree temperature, and she pulled her jacket closer around herself, content to observe the man who had become so much more than a coworker.

Three days since the gala. Three days since their first kiss in front of two hundred people, and she still felt the flutter of butterflies when Parker looked at her with that soft expression that said she mattered to him in ways that went far beyond their professional partnership.

"She's looking good," Shannon called as Parker checked Miracle's legs for any heat or swelling.

"Always does after a day off," Parker replied, glancing up with a smile that made her pulse skip. "Horses are like people. They need time to rest and recover."

When he finished with Miracle and approached the fence where she stood, he laced his fingers with hers, sending tingles up her arm.

"Good morning," he said, leaning closer.

"Good morning yourself," Shannon replied, accepting the gentle kiss he pressed against her lips. Sweet, unhurried, like they had all the time in the world to explore this new territory between them.

As he led her inside the stable, the sharp ring of Parker's cell phone cut through the peacefulness. He frowned, fishing the device from his shirt pocket with obvious reluctance.

"It's Mom," he said, concern flickering across his features as he answered. "Hey, what's—"

Shannon couldn't hear the other side of the conversation, but she saw Parker's eyes narrow as he listened. His shoulders tensed, his free hand fisting at his side.

"Slow down," Parker said, his voice gentler now, soothing. "Tell me what happened."

More unintelligible words came from the phone. Shannon heard the distressed tone, though muffled.

"No, Mom, don't apologize. This isn't your fault." Parker began pacing in small circles, his boots clomping against the textured concrete floor. "When did Brad leave?"

A pause, then Parker's expression darkened.

"This morning? He couldn't give you more notice than that?" Frustration edged his voice. "The water line to the north pasture? How bad is the flooding?"

Shannon's stomach clenched as she pieced together the problem.

"Mom, listen to me," Parker said firmly. "I'm coming up. Today. I can be there by early afternoon if I leave now."

Parker's jaw twitched at whatever his mother said next.

"I don't care if you think you can handle it alone. You shouldn't have to. The forecast shows more snow tonight. You can't be out there trying to fix water lines in a blizzard."

The call ended a few minutes later with promises to drive carefully. When Parker tucked his phone away and turned back to Shannon, his shoulders sagged with the weight of conflicting responsibilities.

"I have to go to Flagstaff," he said. "My mom's in over her head with the ranch, and the kid she had helping her just left for Wyoming for the holidays. She's got a burst water line, probably storm damage, and she's trying to handle it all alone."

"Go," Shannon said without hesitation. "Of course, you have to go help her."

Parker stepped closer, his hands cupping her face with gentle care, calloused fingers warm against her skin.

"I hate the timing," he said. "We are just figuring out what this is between us, and now I have to leave."

She covered his hands with hers, anchoring herself in his touch. "Family comes first. That's one thing I lo—" She caught herself before the word slipped out completely. "One thing I admire most about you."

Warmth flooded Shannon's cheeks under his searching gaze. She'd come too close to declaring feelings too deep and too soon.

"What if I came with you?" The offer sprang from her heart before her mind could filter it. "I mean, if your mom's dealing with storm damage and equipment problems, maybe she could use an extra pair of hands. I grew up helping Aunt Shirley with all kinds of repairs around her property."

"You don't understand. It will not be pretty. Hard physical labor in cold weather, staying in a drafty house."

"We're a good team, remember?" Shannon said, echoing his words from the gala. "Besides, I know which end of a hammer to hold."

A half-smile quirked one side of his mouth while he studied her for a long moment.

"Bringing you home to meet my mother feels like a big step," he mumbled, rubbing a hand over the back of his neck.

She pressed her hand to her stomach as nerves and excitement twisted together. "Would that be such a terrible thing?"

"No," Parker said finally, his smile soft but tinged with worry. "It wouldn't be terrible at all."

Two hours later, after briefly stopping at her apartment in North Phoenix, they climbed into Parker's truck with enough clothes and supplies for a four-day stay. The drive north took them through an increasingly dramatic landscape as the desert floor gave way to mountain switchbacks, then to pine forests dusted with snow.

They spent the first hour talking through what they might find when they arrived—burst water lines, frozen equipment, and storm damage to outbuildings. Parker described the ranch layout, the antiquated water system his father had always meant to upgrade, and the way snow loads could collapse barn roofs if you weren't careful.

"I should probably warn you," Parker said as they climbed higher into the mountains, "my mom can be a bit intense. She's been handling everything alone for three years, so she's gotten used to doing things her way."

"Intense how?" Shannon asked, keeping her tone light.

Parker's hands flexed on the steering wheel. "She has opinions. Strong ones. And she's not shy about sharing them."

"Are you worried she won't like me?"

"No." Parker's answer came quickly, firmly. "I'm worried she'll like you too much, jump to conclusions. Start planning our future before we've even figured out what we're doing."

Shannon's pulse quickened. "What *are* we doing?"

"I don't know yet," Parker admitted. "Do you?"

The honesty in his voice made her throat ache. They were both so careful, both so scared of moving too fast or assuming too much.

"No," she said softly. "But I'd like to find out."

Parker reached across the console and caught her hand, lacing their fingers together. "Me too. Which is why I think maybe we should keep things simple when we get there. Not hide anything, but not make a big production out of it either."

"What does that mean?"

"Maybe just introduce you as a friend from work who

offered to help?" Parker's tone was careful, tentative. "That way Mom doesn't get ahead of herself. Start asking when we're getting married or whether we want kids."

Shannon's stomach flipped at the casual mention of marriage and children, but she understood what he was trying to say. They were too new, too fragile to withstand the weight of family expectations and assumptions.

"So we're friends who help each other," Shannon said. "That's not a lie."

"Exactly." Relief colored Parker's voice. "And if something shifts while we're there, if we need to tell her the truth, we can. But I'd rather not walk into my mother's house and immediately have her analyzing every look between us."

"I can work with that," Shannon agreed, though part of her felt the familiar sting of being kept at arm's length. Yet this differed from her father's emotional distance or Lucas's deception. This was Parker trying to protect their fragile new relationship from the crushing weight of expectations.

They drove in comfortable silence for several miles. The landscape grew whiter as the elevation increased. Snow clung to pine branches and dusted the roadside, creating a winter wonderland that felt worlds away from the Sonoran desert they'd left behind.

"Your turn," Parker said eventually. "Tell me about your family. I know about your mom leaving and Aunt Shirley stepping in, but what about your dad?"

A familiar ache spread through her.

"My father is a good man," she began, choosing her words carefully. "Mining operations manager. He's respected in his field and always provided for me."

"But?" Parker prompted gently.

"But he's emotionally absent." The words came out flat, matter-of-fact, years of practice keeping the hurt locked down. "Always has been. But after Mom left, he threw himself even deeper into work. I think it was easier for him to solve problems at the mine than to deal with his grief. Or mine."

His hand tightened on hers.

"He meant well," she continued. "He made sure I had everything I needed materially. Paid for good schools, gave me spending money, and set up a college fund. But he was never there for the things that mattered to me—school events, birthdays, or even just daily dinner conversation. Work always came first."

"That must have been lonely."

"It taught me to be self-sufficient." She tried for a light tone but couldn't quite manage it. "How to take care of myself. How not to need anyone."

"Is that what you think?" Parker glanced at her, his expression serious. "That needing people is a weakness?"

Shannon stared out the window at the passing pine forest. "I think needing people who aren't there hurts worse than not needing anyone at all."

The truth of it hung between them, raw and vulnerable. This was why she'd built such careful walls around her heart. Her mother had left. Her father had chosen work instead of connection. And Lucas had proven that even when she opened herself to someone, she couldn't trust her instincts about who was safe.

"I get that," Parker said quietly. "After Lucas, after watching my dad enable him for years, I learned to keep people at a distance too. If you don't let anyone close, they can't disappoint you."

"Exactly." Tears pricked her eyes at being understood so completely.

Parker's hand tightened gently on hers. "But I'm tired of it, Shannon. Of being so careful all the time that I miss out on something real."

The vulnerability in his voice cut straight through her defenses.

"Aunt Shirley tells me the same thing. That I'll never find what I'm looking for if I'm too scared to trust anyone."

"Are you? Scared to trust me?"

Shannon looked at their joined hands, at the way his calloused fingers threaded through hers with such careful gentleness. Was she scared? Terrified was more accurate. But she was also here, wasn't she? Driving north to meet his mother, offering to spend four days helping. That had to mean something.

"A little," she admitted. "My dad taught me that even good men can be emotionally unavailable when work matters more than relationships. That dedication to a job can look like dedication to people, but it's not the same thing."

Parker absorbed this, his expression thoughtful. "Is that why you were so hesitant about us at first? You thought I was like your dad?"

"Maybe." Shannon hadn't consciously made the connection, but now that Parker named it, she could see the pattern. Men who worked hard, who took pride in their responsibilities, who seemed reliable—they were also the men who could leave you emotionally stranded while they pursued their own priorities.

"I'm not him," Parker said firmly. "I care about my work, and I take my responsibilities seriously, but you matter more than any job ever could."

The declaration should have brought comfort. Instead, she heard other voices making similar promises. Her mother had promised to always be there. Her father had promised she was his top priority. Lucas had promised her a future built on lies.

"I want to believe that," she whispered, her voice barely audible over the truck's engine. "I'm trying to believe it."

"That's all I'm asking. Just try. We'll figure out the rest as we go."

"I should warn you," Shannon said, needing to be honest even if it scared her. "I'm not good at this. At letting people close, at trusting my instincts about relationships. The last time I thought I'd found something real, I—"

She stopped abruptly, catching herself before she mentioned Lucas by name. That conversation would open wounds she wasn't ready to expose, not here in the cab of Parker's truck while they drove toward his mother's ranch.

"You what?" Parker asked gently.

"I was wrong about someone," Shannon finished carefully. "Someone I trusted, someone I thought cared about me. It turned out I'd misread everything, seen what I wanted to see instead of who they really were."

"That's not a character flaw in you," he said. "That's someone else taking advantage of your trust."

"Maybe." She traced the edge of the window with her finger, watching frost patterns form on the glass. "But it made me question everything. My judgment, my instincts, my ability to tell the difference between genuine connection and manipulation."

Parker was quiet for a long moment. When he spoke, his voice carried a sympathetic tone.

"Shannon, you can't let one person's betrayal steal your ability to see the good in others."

"Says the man who wants to introduce me as just a friend to his mother," Shannon pointed out, though she kept her tone gentle.

Parker winced. "That's fair. I'm asking you to trust me while I'm being careful about how much I trust this situation."

"I'm not criticizing," she said quickly. "I understand being cautious. I just want us to be honest about what we're both doing—protecting ourselves because we've been hurt before."

"There," Parker said suddenly, pointing to a wooden sign at the turnoff. "Walnut Canyon Ranch. Home sweet home."

As the truck slowed, something cold crept over Shannon's skin. Not from the cold air seeping through the vents, but from the landscape itself. The curve of the road between two massive boulders. The slope of the hills. The way the pine trees framed the valley.

Her throat tightened.

"Parker," she said, voice thin and distant. "What did you say the name was?"

"Walnut Canyon Ranch," he repeated, glancing at her with concern. "Why? You look like you've seen a ghost."

She stared at the gravel drive winding between snow-dusted fence posts. The rusted gate with its weathered wood frame. The way the road curved toward a house she couldn't quite see yet but somehow knew would be tucked against the hillside.

Her pulse thudded in her ears, each beat echoing with recognition she didn't want to claim.

"Shannon?" Parker's voice sounded distant, like it came through water. "What's wrong?"

She opened her mouth, but the words tangled in the rush of memory. Cold recognition gripped her chest, squeezing until she could barely breathe.

"I know this place."

They rounded the last bend, and the ranch house came into view—weathered siding, dark roof, windows overlooking the pastures blanketed in thick snow. She had completely forgotten about it. After Lucas's betrayal, she'd tried to erase every moment with him.

"Lucas brought me here once."

The words cut loose a flood of memories, sharp and unrelenting. They crashed through her like monsoon runoff, threatening to sweep away everything she'd begun to build with the man beside her.

———

Parker stared at Shannon, her words echoing in his mind like a stone dropped into still water, sending ripples through everything he thought he understood about his life.

The familiar outline of the ranch house, the corrals, even the mountains in the distance seemed to shift and blur.

"He brought you here," he said, his voice coming out flat.

Shannon's face had gone pale, her dark eyes wide. She nodded slowly, her hands clutching the truck's grab bar.

"Lucas brought me here," she whispered. "Eight years ago. During those six months we dated."

The air left Parker's lungs. Lucas had brought her here. To Walnut Canyon Ranch. To their mother.

His throat burned. "He brought you to meet Mom."

"She was so kind to me," Shannon continued, her voice breaking slightly. "Made this incredible dinner, showed me photo albums, told me stories about him growing up. She was proud of him, but she worried about Lucas. Said he was too charming for his own good. That he needed someone steady to help him find his way."

Parker's hands tightened on the steering wheel, knuckles going white. His mother had loved Shannon. Had probably already picked out names for grandchildren. Had seen her as—

He cut off the thought, but his stomach kept churning. Shannon had been welcomed here, had sat at their table, had listened to his mother's stories. And then Lucas had stolen from her and vanished.

"Parker?" Shannon's voice sounded far away. "Are you okay?"

He wasn't okay. The one place that had always been his, and Lucas's shadow was already here. Waiting.

He jammed the shifter into park and cut the engine, but couldn't bring himself to move. His hand lingered on the key, fingers frozen.

The front door opened, cutting through his spiraling thoughts. Parker looked up to see his mother stepping onto the porch, her silver hair pulled back in the same practical bun she'd worn for as long as he could remember. She wore faded jeans and one of his father's old work shirts. Her weathered hands shaded her eyes as she squinted toward the truck.

"Parker James Quaid," she called, her voice carrying the authority that had ruled his childhood. "Get yourself up here and explain why you brought this weather with you."

He opened his truck door and stepped out. His mother's gaze darted to Shannon emerging from the passenger side.

Her expression shifted. Recognition, then something cold that turned his stomach to lead.

"Well," his mother said, her voice dropping to a tone he knew too well. The same one she'd used after Lucas's last arrest. "If it isn't Shannon Burke."

Shannon froze beside the truck, what little color remained draining from her face. "Mrs. Quaid. I—"

"Didn't expect to see you again," his mother interrupted, her arms crossing over her chest. "Especially not with my *other* son."

Her emphasis twisted something inside Parker. He moved to Shannon's side, his hand finding the small of her back.

"Mom, Shannon is—"

"I know exactly who she is," his mother cut him off, her gray eyes hard as flint. "She's the girl who broke Lucas's heart and sent him running to who knows where. The girl who made him so desperate to prove himself worthy that he started making even worse choices."

Parker's jaw clenched. "That's not what happened, and you know it."

"Do I?" His mother's laugh was bitter. "All I know is Lucas brought her home, talked about marriage and settling down and maybe taking over the ranch someday. Then she left, and he fell apart completely. Started getting into worse trouble than ever before."

"Mrs. Quaid," Shannon said, her voice steady despite the tremor Parker could feel running through her body. "Lucas stole my college money. He's the one who—"

"So you say." His mother's tone could have frozen fire. "But my son loved you. And you threw it back in his face."

Parker's vision blurred red around the edges. His chest felt too tight, his breath coming shallow. Shannon had been Lucas's victim, not his destroyer. She'd been twenty years old and trusting and had nearly lost everything because of his brother's lies.

But his mother wasn't seeing that. She was seeing— what? The girl who could've saved Lucas? The daughter-in-law who got away?

Parker didn't know. He just knew his mother was looking at Shannon with the same wounded anger she'd worn for years every time Lucas's name came up.

"We need to get inside," he said, his voice rougher than he'd intended. "Shannon's exhausted, and we both need to warm up."

His mother's gaze flicked between them, taking in their proximity, the way he stood beside Shannon. Her mouth thinned.

"I suppose you expect me to make up the guest room," she said.

"Please," Parker replied, though part of him wanted to load Shannon back in the truck and drive through the storm rather than subject her to this.

"I don't have the energy to make up another room," Mom said flatly. "You'll have to do it yourself."

The words stung. In all his years growing up, his mother had never failed to welcome guests with warmth and generosity. Not once.

Before he could respond, his mother's brows drew together.

"Right now I need you to deal with that water line to the stock tanks," she said. "Been gushing for three hours, and I can't get it to shut off. Water's flooding the entire area around the tanks, and if this keeps up, we'll lose the whole watering system. The UTV's got tools. Parked out back."

Parker's heart sank. The storm, the freezing temperatures, the age of the ranch's watering system—he could already see the damage in his mind. Thousands of dollars if he got to it now. Tens of thousands if he didn't.

He turned toward Shannon, and his gut clenched. She hugged her arms around her middle. He didn't want to put her behind the ranch's needs. Just like her father.

"I have to deal with this," he said, hating every word. "If I don't get that water stopped, we could lose the whole system."

Shannon nodded, her composure intact despite everything. "Of course. Do what you need to do."

But Parker could see the cost of that composure in the tight line of her shoulders, the careful way she held herself as if bracing for another blow. He was about to leave her alone with a woman who blamed her for Lucas's downward spiral.

His feet felt rooted to the ground. The ranch needed him. Shannon needed him.

He couldn't do both.

"Shannon," he started, not sure what he could say that would make this better.

"Go," she said. "The ranch comes first. I understand."

The resignation in her tone made his chest ache.

"Mom," Parker said, forcing himself to look at the woman who'd raised him, searching for some trace of the warmth he remembered from childhood. "Shannon is important to me. More important than you know. Please—"

"I'll show her where things are," his mother interrupted. Her tone made it clear she'd do it out of duty, nothing more. "Now go fix that pipe before we lose the whole place."

Parker hesitated, his hand still resting on Shannon's back. She stood strong despite being surrounded by hostility and painful memories.

But water was still gushing. Every minute meant more

damage.

"I'll be back as soon as I can," he promised Shannon, his hand squeezing hers briefly. He held on a moment longer than necessary, his thumb brushing across her knuckles.

Then he forced himself to step away.

He glanced back once before heading around the house. Shannon was following his mother through the front door, her back straight and her chin raised.

Parker climbed into the UTV and headed toward the pasture, his hands gripping the steering wheel tight enough to hurt. Some floods could be stopped with quick action and the right tools.

Others drowned everything in their path.

13

SHANNON STOOD IN the doorway of the Quaid ranch house, her overnight bag clutched in her hands as memories she'd buried for years clawed their way to the surface. The scent of coffee and faint traces of cigarette smoke—long since aired out but somehow still lingering in the fabric of the place—transported her back to a twenty-year-old girl who'd believed in forever with a charming boy who'd brought her to this very house.

Lucas had stood in this exact doorway, his arm around her shoulders, promising her a false future that existed only in his imagination. She'd met his parents in this living room, had shared meals at that kitchen table, had foolishly let herself dream of belonging somewhere after a childhood of being shuffled between her father's work obligations and her great-aunt's busy life.

Her chest tightened, but she forced herself to breathe slowly. She wasn't that naïve girl anymore. She was a woman who'd rebuilt her life, who'd learned to trust carefully but completely when someone proved worthy. And Parker— Parker was nothing like his twin.

Lord, help me be gracious here. Help me see Joanna through Your eyes, not through the lens of my past hurt. And please, keep Parker safe with whatever's happening out there.

"Well," Joanna said, her voice carrying a chill that could

frost windows in July. "I suppose you'll be wanting the guest room."

The woman stood rigid beside the stone fireplace, her gray hair pulled back in a severe bun, her faded jeans and flannel shirt practical rather than welcoming. Everything about her posture screamed suspicion, and Shannon couldn't blame her. If their positions were reversed, if someone connected to Lucas showed up on her doorstep claiming to care about Parker, she'd be suspicious too.

"Whatever works best for you, Mrs. Quaid," Shannon replied, keeping her tone respectful. "I don't want to impose."

Joanna's laugh was bitter. "Impose? Honey, you being here at all is an imposition. But Parker seems to think you're different from —" She stopped herself, pressing her lips into a thin line. "Doesn't matter what I think, I suppose."

The unfinished comparison hung in the air between them. Different from Lucas. The words might as well have been carved in stone.

Joanna moved toward the front door, grabbing a heavy work coat from a peg on the wall. "I need to go check on the horses, make sure whatever spooked them didn't cause any real damage. You can..." She gestured vaguely toward the living room. "Make yourself at home, I guess."

The door closed behind her with more force than necessary, leaving Shannon alone in the sudden quiet. She set her bag down and wrapped her arms around herself, the silence almost oppressive after the emotional weight of the past few minutes.

Being here hurt. She hadn't expected it to hurt this much.

But as she stood there, surrounded by Parker's childhood home, Shannon felt something shift inside her. This wasn't Lucas's space anymore. It was Parker's. The man who'd bid his entire savings to give her something she'd lost, who'd shown her what genuine love looked like through actions rather than empty promises.

She could choose to let the past paralyze her, or she could choose to honor the present.

Shannon picked up her bag and headed down the hallway, noting the family photos lining the walls. Parker at various ages—gap-toothed grins, Little League uniforms, graduation pictures. And Lucas, identical in appearance but somehow different even in still photographs. Where Parker's smiles seemed genuine, Lucas's had an edge of performance, as if he were already calculating his next move.

The guest room was small, with a double bed covered in a faded quilt and a dresser that had seen better decades. Shannon's gaze automatically scanned the space. Faded rectangles on the wall marked where posters had once hung. A single nail hole near the window suggested a pennant or banner. The closet door hung slightly ajar, revealing empty hangers that somehow felt like ghosts.

Her breath caught as understanding slammed into her chest like a physical blow. This had been Lucas's room.

Shannon's hands began to tremble, her overnight bag slipping from nerveless fingers to thud against the hardwood floor. The sound echoed in the small space, hollow and final. She pressed her palm against the door frame, needing something solid to anchor her as memories flooded back. Lucas had laughed as he showed her his childhood bedroom, spinning stories about the posters he'd collected, the dreams he'd claimed to have.

All lies. Even then, in this very room, he'd been practicing the charm that would later destroy her life.

The walls seemed to close in, suffocating her with a fresh wave of betrayal. How many nights had Lucas slept in this bed, planning his next con? How many times had he stood at this window, calculating which hearts to break next?

Had Joanna done this deliberately? Put her in the room that belonged to the man who'd stolen everything from her? Or was Shannon reading malice where none was intended?

Lord, I need You. I don't know whether I can do this. Give me strength to stay, to honor Parker by being here. Don't let the past win by driving me away from the man I love.

Shannon forced herself to breathe slowly, in and out, until her hands steadied enough to strip the sheets from the bed. The linens fell to the floor in a heap, taking with them whatever traces of Lucas might have lingered. She would make this space hers, if only for a few nights. She would not let the past control her choices.

Rummaging through the hall closet, she found a duster. She returned to the guest room and ran the duster over the furniture and decor before proceeding to Parker's room.

The door was ajar, revealing rodeo posters on the walls and a Phoenix Suns pennant hanging above a twin bed that looked like it hadn't been slept in for months. This was harder—touching his personal space, seeing the remnants of the boy who'd grown into the honorable man.

Shannon changed the sheets and straightened the few items on his dresser. A framed photo of Parker with an older man—his father, she realized—both of them grinning beside a massive bay horse. A basketball signed by players she didn't recognize but who'd obviously meant something to a teenage Parker. A silver dollar that looked like it had been polished smooth by countless handling.

Each item told a story of a boy who'd been loved, who'd had dreams and heroes and simple pleasures. So different from the criminal his twin had become.

With both bedrooms tidied, Shannon made her way to the kitchen. The refrigerator was well-stocked but in the way of someone who shopped efficiently rather than enthusiastically. Cubed beef that needed to be used soon, vegetables that were fresh, pantry staples for practical meals rather than culinary adventures.

She could work with this.

Shannon found an apron hanging on a hook beside the stove. It was faded blue with tiny white flowers, probably

Joanna's. She tied it around her waist and got to work. Cooking in someone else's kitchen felt both presumptuous and necessary. Joanna might not want her here, but she would not let the woman come home to an empty kitchen after dealing with ranch emergencies.

The scent of browning beef soon filled the kitchen as Shannon started a beef stew. It was a homey meal without being pretentious. While the meat cooked, she peeled potatoes, diced them, and added them to the pot. After chopping the vegetables, she dumped them in too.

As she cleaned up the kitchen, she tried not to think about how many times Lucas had sat at this same table, charming his parents with lies they'd desperately wanted to believe. Or how many times Parker suffered in private silence for his twin's mistakes.

The living room needed attention too, she realized. Not because it was messy, but because it felt abandoned — newspapers stacked haphazardly, throw pillows that had lost their fluff, a coffee table that needed more than just dusting. Shannon straightened without rearranging, respecting the established order while bringing life back to neglected spaces.

When the front door opened, Shannon had just finished dropping pre-made biscuits onto a cookie sheet. Her pulse quickened as she set them aside.

"What in the—"

Joanna's voice carried from the living room, surprise overtaking the earlier hostility. She heard her moving through the house, footsteps pausing at what must be the guest room, then continuing to Parker's room.

"Shannon?" Then Joanna's voice came from the kitchen doorway.

She turned, wooden spoon still in hand from stirring the stew. Joanna's brows shot up, mouth slack, gaze locked on Shannon. Her lips parted as if to speak, but no words came. Her gaze swept the tidy kitchen, lingering on the stew, the savory aromas wafting through the air.

"I hope you don't mind," Shannon said. "I made up rooms for Parker and myself—separate rooms," she added, making sure that point was clear. "And I started dinner. The beef needed to be used, and I thought you might be hungry after dealing with whatever happened outside."

Joanna stood frozen in the doorway, her face cycling through emotions Shannon couldn't quite read. Suspicion was still there, along with something that might have been gratitude.

"You didn't have to do this," Joanna said finally, her tone carefully neutral.

"I know," Shannon replied, turning back to the simmering stew. "But I wanted to help. Is everything okay with the horses?"

"False alarm. Stray dog." Joanna's voice remained guarded. "Parker's still fixing the water system."

Shannon nodded absently as she slid the biscuits into the oven. "This just needs fifteen minutes in the oven, and it'll be ready."

Then she began washing the dishes she'd used. The silence stretched between them, heavy with unspoken questions and years of complicated history.

Joanna watched her for another moment, her expression unreadable. "Smells good," she said finally, the words carrying neither warmth nor coldness. Only acknowledgment.

Then she turned and walked back toward the living room, leaving Shannon alone with her uncertainty and the ticking of the oven timer.

Shannon dried her hands on the dish towel, staring at the empty doorway where Joanna had been. Outside, the wind howled against the windows. She wrapped her arms around herself and tried not to think about how far she was from anywhere that felt like safety.

She'd chosen to come here. Chosen to walk back into the place where Lucas had spun his lies. Now all she could do was wait and see if grace could grow in ground that had been poisoned by betrayal.

———

PARKER'S BOOTS SLIPPED on the ice-slicked ground around the water tank, his arms windmilling as he fought to keep his balance. Three hours of steady leaking had turned the area into a treacherous skating rink, the escaping water freezing almost as fast as it hit the winter air.

The metal wrench felt like it weighed fifty pounds in his numb fingers as he cranked the emergency shutoff valve one last turn. The frigid wind sliced through his coat, carrying the scent of impending snow and the bitter promise that this storm wasn't finished with them yet.

The gushing water finally stopped, leaving behind an eerie quiet broken only by the wind howling across the north pasture. Parker surveyed the damage. A four-inch section of copper pipe that had burst when the temperature dropped too fast for the water inside to drain properly. Ice crystals clung to the twisted metal like frozen tears.

Three hours. Three hours of driving out here in the UTV, then slipping and sliding on ice while carrying tools that grew heavier with each step. Three hours of crawling around the tank housing in frozen mud, chipping ice away from fittings.

Three hours of trying not to think about what was happening inside his house, where his mother and Shannon were trapped together like two wildcats in a cage.

Parker pulled out his phone with stiff fingers, squinting at the screen through the gray afternoon light. His thumbs barely cooperated as he typed out a message to Adan.

Need prayer. Water emergency fixed for now, but Mom and Shannon have been alone for hours. Pray this doesn't end in disaster.

The response came back almost immediately. *Already*

praying, brother. "The Lord is far from the wicked, but he hears the prayer of the righteous." Proverbs 15:29. God's got this.

Righteous. There was that word again.

Parker stared at the verse, his breath forming clouds in the frigid air as the wind tried to steal his phone from his numb fingers. He'd been having this conversation with his friend for days now, ever since that first Bible study at the bunkhouse. The word had stuck in his throat like a fishbone when Adan first used it, so foreign to how Parker saw himself that he'd actually laughed.

"What's so funny?" Adan had asked, genuine curiosity in his voice.

"You called us righteous. Me and you. That's not exactly how I'd describe myself."

Adan had set down his coffee, leaning forward with the patient expression he wore when explaining something important. "Morally upright. Without guilt or sin. That's what righteous means."

"How do you figure that applies to either of us?" Parker had shot back. "I mean, I get that you're a good man, Adan, but righteous? That's Sunday school perfect, not real world broken."

"It applies to me," Adan had said, not with arrogance but with a humble certainty that made Parker want to understand. "Not because I'm perfect, but because Jesus died, taking on my sins so I could become righteous. His righteousness becomes mine."

The words still echoed in Parker's mind as he fired up the small torch he'd brought, the blue flame hissing as he began heating the coupling for his temporary repair. The heat felt good, even as the acrid smell of melting flux made his eyes water. He fed solder into the joint, watching the silver metal flow and seal the connection that would have to hold until spring.

How could a man be free from guilt when guilt lived in his gut like a permanent resident? Guilt for hating his brother with a ferocity that sometimes scared him. Guilt for running away from Walnut Canyon Ranch when his mother needed him most. Guilt for trying to carve out his own life at Vargas Ranch when he should be home, patching his family's ranch back together, helping Mom survive.

No, Parker didn't feel morally upright. Maybe a little better than Lucas, but that was setting the bar pretty low. Not to the point of calling himself righteous.

But Adan kept saying God heard the prayers of the righteous, and if that was true, maybe his desperate plea for peace between the two women he loved most might actually reach God's ears.

The solder cooled and hardened, creating a seal that should hold through the winter. Parker turned off the torch and tested the connection with gentle pressure. It held. The repair wasn't pretty, but it would keep the cattle watered until he could arrange for a more permanent fix.

The wind gusted harder, reminding Parker that standing in an ice storm contemplating theology was a luxury he couldn't afford. He needed to warm up before hypothermia became an issue.

He stowed the torch and tools in the box in the back of the UTV before driving back to the barn. Once inside, the barn felt like a tropical paradise compared to the frozen wasteland outside. Parker cranked up the space heater in the office and stood directly in front of it, letting the warm air thaw his face while he rubbed feeling back into his hands. Horses whuffled from their cozy stalls. The familiar scents of leather and hay provided comfort, grounding him in the routine normalcy of ranch life.

When the tingling in his fingers subsided, he made his way through the barn, checking on the animals out of habit more than necessity. The horses looked comfortable, with their water buckets full and hay nets topped off. Parker frowned, moving to the feed room to check the schedule posted on the wall.

Evening feeding wasn't supposed to happen for another hour, but clearly someone had already taken care of it. The grain buckets were washed and stacked, and the hay net fillers were put away properly. Even the barn aisle had been swept, something that usually waited until morning.

His phone buzzed again. Another text from Adan: *Remember what we talked about. You can't control Lucas or your mom or what happens. But you can trust God with the people you love. And the ones you struggle to love.*

Trust God. Easy for Adan to say. Adan didn't have a brother who destroyed everything he touched. Adan's mother didn't blame him for every family crisis that had occurred since birth.

But maybe that was the point. Maybe trust wasn't about having perfect circumstances. Maybe it was about believing God could work even when everything felt broken.

Parker moved to the last stall, where their old gelding Tucker stood contentedly munching hay. Someone had even brushed him down, his winter coat shining despite the cold. The thoroughness of the care told him this hadn't been a rushed job. Someone had spent time here, had done the work with the same attention to detail he would have given it himself.

Mom, probably. She'd always been good with the animals, had probably used the barn chores as an excuse to get away from whatever awkwardness was brewing in the house. Although the thought of Shannon Burke—city nonprofit executive in her nice clothes—mucking stalls and hauling water buckets sent an unexpected flutter through his chest.

With nothing else needing his attention, Parker turned off the space heater in the office. Time to face whatever waited inside the house. He steeled himself as he crunched through the snow toward the back door, mentally preparing for the worst-case scenario. Shouting voices. Tears. His mother's cold fury and Shannon's wounded retreat. Maybe

Shannon had already packed her bags and called for a ride back to Phoenix, unwilling to endure another minute of Mom's hostility.

Parker paused at the door, his hand on the knob, and offered up what might have been the most honest prayer of his life. *God, if You really do hear prayers, if Adan's right about any of this, please don't let Mom have destroyed this. Shannon doesn't deserve to pay for Lucas's sins. Neither of us do.*

The prayer felt odd, unfamiliar. Yet, he should have been doing it all along instead of trying to manage everything through sheer willpower and careful planning.

When he opened the door, warmth wrapped around him like an embrace. The kitchen smelled of something wonderful—coffee and beef stew and warmth that made his stomach remember he'd skipped lunch in his rush to fix the water lines. But more than that, the house seemed... quiet. Not a simmering quiet waiting to explode, but not entirely peaceful either. Careful.

He pulled off his boots and hung his coat on the hook by the door, listening for voices. Nothing. The silence stretched, making him wonder if Shannon had retreated to her room to avoid further confrontation.

"Mom?" he called softly.

"In here," came the reply from the living room, her tone giving nothing away.

Parker found his mother sitting in her usual chair, hands folded in her lap, staring out the window at the swirling snow. Shannon was nowhere to be seen.

"Where's Shannon?"

"Guest room. Said she wanted to rest before dinner." Mom's voice was carefully neutral. "Stew's ready when you are."

He studied his mother's profile, trying to read the emotions she kept so carefully controlled. "How did it go?"

Mom was quiet for a long moment, her gaze still fixed on the storm outside. "She made herself useful. Cleaned up, made dinner, was respectful."

"That's good, right?"

"She's trying," Mom said, finally turning to face him. Her eyes were sharp, not angry, just watchful. "But I've seen people try for all the wrong reasons."

Parker frowned. "What does that mean?"

"It means I don't trust easy. Not when someone shows up out of nowhere with a history like hers." Her voice softened, but the edge remained. "She dated your brother, Parker. And now she's here with you. That's not nothing."

"She didn't come here for Lucas," he said quickly. "She came to help."

"Maybe. Or maybe she came because you look just like the man who broke her heart." Mom stood and walked toward the kitchen, her movements precise. "You ever think about that? About what it means to be the twin of someone who hurt her?"

Parker followed, the weight of her words pressing down. "She's not using me."

"You sure?" She turned, one hand on the cabinet door. "Because from where I'm standing, it looks like she's trying real hard to prove something. To herself. To me. Maybe even to Lucas, wherever he is."

"She's not like that," Parker said, quieter now.

"I hope not." Mom pulled two bowls from the cabinet. "But you've known her a month. That's not long enough to know if someone's here for you or for what you represent."

"She chose to come here," he said. "Knowing it would be hard."

"Sometimes people choose hard things because they want something out of them." She ladled stew into the bowls, her voice steady. "Closure. Control. A second chance at rewriting the past. Just make sure you're not the pen she's using."

Before Parker could respond, footsteps echoed down the hall. Shannon appeared in the kitchen doorway, hair smoothed, composure intact.

"Perfect timing," Shannon said, her smile not quite reaching her eyes.

Parker inhaled deeply as he scrubbed his hands in the sink. "Something smells incredible in here."

Mom ladled stew into bowls without looking up. "Just beef stew and biscuits. Nothing fancy."

"Smells perfect to me," Parker said, accepting his bowl gratefully.

They gathered around the kitchen table in careful silence, the only sounds were the clink of spoons against ceramic and the wind rattling the windows. The weight of unspoken words hung heavy in the room.

"This is really good," he said finally, trying to break the tension.

"Shannon made it," Mom said, the words carrying neither praise nor criticism. "Found things in the pantry I'd forgotten about."

"I just worked with what was available," Shannon replied.

The conversation settled into a careful politeness, each of them focused on their bowls. The refrigerator hummed in the corner. From the edge of his vision, Parker watched both women. Mom's shoulders no longer braced like armor. Shannon no longer glanced toward the door as if plotting her exit. When Mom quietly asked Shannon to pass the salt, it felt like a small miracle.

Maybe God had answered part of his prayer after all. Shannon was still here, still willing to endure his mother's suspicion for his sake. Mom hadn't driven her away or said anything unforgivable. It wasn't the miraculous reconciliation he'd hoped for, but it was grace enough to get through the night.

"I should clean up," Shannon said, rising to gather the bowls.

"I'll help," Parker offered, but Mom waved him off.

"You've been outside in the cold for hours. Go warm up. We can handle the dishes."

As Parker headed toward the living room, he caught the tail end of Mom's quiet words to Shannon.

"Was the guest room warm enough?"

"Yes, thank you."

Parker froze in the hallway, the implication hitting him like ice water. The guest room. Of course, Shannon would need her own room. He wouldn't have it any other way. But the guest room wasn't just any room.

It was Lucas's old room.

Nausea clawed up his throat. His twin's room. The same bed where Lucas had slept as a teenager, planning cons and perfecting lies. The same walls that had witnessed him bragging about his latest mark, his newest victim. Shannon—sweet, trusting Shannon, who'd already suffered enough at Lucas's hands—would lay her head on a pillow his brother had used.

The wrongness of it made Parker's skin crawl. She was his now. His heart, his hope, his chance at something real and good. But here, in this house, surrounded by Lucas's memory, how could she be anything but his brother's cast-off? The girl Lucas had stolen from now sought comfort with his identical twin.

The thought hit him like a physical blow. Was that all he'd ever be to her? A replacement? A way to rewrite the ending Lucas had stolen from her?

Parker's hands fisted at his sides. His mother had done this deliberately. He was certain of it. Mom, who still kept Lucas's football trophies on the shelf, who'd never quite forgiven the world for failing to save her golden boy. She'd put Shannon in that room as a reminder—to Shannon, to Parker, to everyone—of who belonged here first.

The cruelty of it stole his breath. Shannon had come here with noble intentions, to stand beside him when his family needed help. And Mom had repaid that kindness by forcing her to sleep in the room of the man destroyed her life.

But worse than his mother's calculated coldness was the poisonous doubt now sluicing through his veins. Would Shannon look at that room and remember Lucas's voice, Lucas's promises? Would she lie awake comparing twins, wondering if Parker carried the same capacity for betrayal hidden behind an identical appearance?

He sank into the living room chair, staring at the family photos on the mantel. Pictures of him and Lucas at various ages, remembering how they'd fooled teachers, neighbors, even their own relatives. But never their parents. Mom had always known which twin was which, had always loved Lucas more fiercely, more desperately.

Maybe she was right to put Shannon there. Maybe it was time Shannon faced the truth—that Parker would always be Lucas's shadow, the second choice, the consolation prize for what she'd really wanted.

The storm outside rattled the windows and whistled through the tiny gap around the doorframe, but it was nothing compared to the tempest in his soul. Tomorrow would bring another day of his mother's tests, of Shannon's careful politeness, of all of them pretending this wasn't about Lucas when everything was always about Lucas.

Parker closed his eyes, his prayer more desperate than faithful. *God, if You're listening, if any of this means anything — help me know if I'm just fooling myself. Help me see if Shannon could ever really choose me, or if I'm just the safe version of the man who broke her heart.*

For now, Shannon slept in Lucas's room, and Parker sat alone with the growing certainty that some shadows were too long to escape.

14

SHANNON'S EYES FLEW open as the wind howled outside. She exhaled and sank back into the pillow, her gaze drifting to the pale gray light seeping through faded curtains. Their once-bold pattern faded to the pale outline of flowers.

Where was she?

The unfamiliar ceiling came into focus. Right. The ranch. Parker's ranch.

She swallowed, but her throat didn't cooperate — tight and scratchy, like she'd been breathing dust. Or holding back words. Or both.

Lucas's room. She'd slept in Lucas's childhood bedroom, surrounded by the ghosts of his lies and the echoes of promises he'd never intended to keep. But as she sat up and pulled on her warmest clothes, Shannon made a deliberate choice. This was Parker's family home now. Parker's life. Parker's mother, who needed help with a struggling ranch.

She was here for Parker, not to wage war with the unchangeable past.

The house was quiet as she crept down the hall, the old floorboards creaking softly under her feet. Through the kitchen window, she could see the barn in the distance, a warm yellow glow spilling from the windows where someone was already working despite the early hour. Parker most likely started the morning chores that kept a ranch running.

Shannon pulled on her coat and boots, wrapping a scarf around her neck before stepping into the bitter air. The snow had stopped during the night, leaving behind a world transformed into crystalline beauty. Each fence post wore a cap of white, and the pastures stretched endlessly under a blanket sparkling in the weak morning sun.

Her breath formed clouds as she trudged through the snow toward the barn, following the path Parker's boots had carved earlier. The cold bit at her cheeks and made her eyes water, but it felt clean, honest in a way that cut through the emotional fog of yesterday.

"Morning," she called softly as she stepped through the barn door, stomping snow from her boots.

Parker looked up from the stall where he was forking fresh hay, surprise flickering across his features. "You're up early."

"City habits," Shannon said with a smile that felt more genuine than it had yesterday. "Besides, I figured you could use some help."

Something shifted in Parker's expression. He gestured toward the feed room with his chin.

"Grain buckets are in there if you want to start with the horses on the left side. Two scoops each, except for the old mare in the third stall. She only gets one."

Shannon nodded, rolling up her sleeves despite the cold. Parker had shown her the routine down at Vargas Ranch one morning a few weeks ago. It came back quickly. Measure, pour, move to the next stall. The horses nickered softly as she approached, their warm breath creating small clouds in the frigid air.

The work felt good, purposeful, and grounding. With each bucket of grain, each gentle word to a curious horse, Shannon settled more firmly into this present moment rather than the painful past that seemed to lurk in every corner of this place.

"Thank you," Parker said quietly when they met in the center aisle, both carrying empty buckets. "For being here. For helping."

"Where else would I be?" Shannon replied, meaning it wholeheartedly.

The sound of the barn door opening interrupted their moment of connection. Joanna Quaid stepped inside, her silver hair pulled back in a practical bun, her weathered face set in lines that suggested she'd slept about as well as Shannon had.

"Morning," she said, her tone carefully neutral as her gaze moved between them.

"Mrs. Quaid," Shannon replied with the same polite distance they'd maintained yesterday. "I hope we didn't wake you."

"I've been getting up before dawn for forty years," Joanna said, moving toward the tack room. "Takes more than a little noise to disturb me."

Parker's mother pulled halters from their pegs, looped lead ropes with practiced flicks of her wrist. She moved between the tack room and stalls like she could do it blindfolded—probably had, at some point. Each halter landed on the right hook. Each rope coiled just so.

Shannon leaned against the barn wall. The woman didn't fuss or fumble. She just... knew. Knew which horse needed what. Knew where everything belonged. Knew these animals the way some people knew their own kids.

"I can help with turnout," she offered, recognizing the next phase of morning chores.

Joanna paused, studying Shannon with those sharp gray eyes that missed nothing. "You know about horses?"

"Some," Shannon said honestly. "I spent summers helping my great-aunt with her property. Different scale than this, but the basics are the same."

"Take Maple," Joanna said finally, handing Shannon a halter. "She's the bay mare in the fourth stall. Easy to handle, but she likes to take her time."

Shannon accepted the halter, heading toward Maple's stall. The mare greeted her with a soft whicker, dark eyes curious but calm as Shannon slipped the halter over her head and clipped on the lead rope.

"There you go, pretty girl," Shannon murmured, stroking Maple's neck. "Ready for some fresh air?"

Leading Maple through the barn toward the pasture gate, Shannon was aware of Joanna watching her every move. Not exactly with hostility, but with careful attention.

The mare stepped carefully through the snow, following Shannon's lead without resistance. At the gate, she waited while Parker opened it, then led Maple through into the pasture where she could stretch her legs.

"She likes you," he observed as they watched Maple amble toward the hay feeder.

"I like her too," she said, meaning it. There was something peaceful about working with animals, about the honest exchange of care for trust that had nothing to do with manipulation or hidden agendas.

They worked in comfortable rhythm after that, leading horses to pasture while Joanna checked water tanks and filled hay nets. Shannon fell into the familiar partnership she and Parker had developed at Vargas Ranch—anticipating each other's movements, sharing the load without needing extensive conversation.

When the last horse had been turned out, they gathered in the barn office, where a small space heater fought against the high country cold. Parker poured coffee from a thermos he'd brought from the house, the rich aroma filling the small space.

"You didn't have to get up this early," Parker said, handing Shannon a steaming cup. "I could have handled the chores alone."

"I wanted to help," Shannon replied, wrapping her hands around the warm ceramic. "Besides, I like this part of ranch life. It's honest work."

Parker's smile was soft, grateful. "I was worried yesterday might have been too much. That you'd want to leave."

Shannon contemplated her words, aware that Joanna was within earshot, organizing bridles on the tack room wall. She wanted to be honest without creating more tension.

"It was hard," she admitted. "Being here brings back memories I'd rather not revisit. But Parker, I'm not here because of the past. I'm here because of the present. Because of you."

Parker blew out a loud breath, his shoulders dropping as he rolled his neck from side to side. He stepped closer and reached for her hand, his calloused fingers warm against hers.

"I know this is complicated," he said. "My family, this place, all the history that lives here. But having you here, seeing you fit into this life means everything to me."

Shannon's throat tightened at the vulnerability in his voice. This strong, steady man, who'd weathered so much, offered his heart despite the risk, despite the complications that could arise from their shared connection to Lucas.

"We're going to be okay," she said, as much for herself as for him. "Whatever comes, we'll face it together."

The sound of tools being organized grew louder from the tack room. Parker's jaw twitched, and his gaze flicked toward the doorway before settling back on her face. She squeezed his hand. Whatever was going on between him and his mother, it wasn't her place to fix. But she could be here. That much she could do.

"I should probably get back to the house," she said, finishing her coffee. "Start some breakfast."

"Shannon," he said as she moved toward the door. "Thank you. For staying. For choosing to be here despite everything."

She turned back, studying his face in the pale morning

light filtering through the barn windows. The worry lines around his eyes, the careful way he held himself as if bracing for disappointment.

"I love you," she said, the words slipping out before she could stop them.

Parker's breath caught, his eyes widening with surprise and something that looked like wonder. "Shannon—"

"I know it's complicated," she continued, her heart racing but her voice steady. "I know there are things we still need to work through. But I needed you to know, whatever happens, whatever challenges we face, that will not change."

The confession hung in the air between them, honest and vulnerable and absolutely true. Shannon had spent eight years guarding her heart, and here she was, offering it completely to a man who carried the same appearance as her betrayer but possessed the soul of someone entirely different.

"I love you too," Parker whispered, crossing the small space between them to cup her face in his hands. "More than I thought I could love anyone."

The kiss was gentle, sweet, carrying the promise of everything they were building together despite the obstacles in their path. When they broke apart, both breathing unsteadily, she rested her hand on his day-old stubble.

"Now go fix whatever else needs fixing around here," she said with a smile. "I'll handle the domestic front."

As Shannon walked back toward the house through the snow, she felt lighter than she had since arriving at Walnut Canyon Ranch. The declaration of love hadn't been planned, but it felt right. Whatever storms they faced—from his mother's skepticism, from the heartache of the past, from whatever future challenges awaited—they would face them with honesty and commitment.

She paused at the kitchen door, looking back toward the barn where Parker was probably already absorbed in the next task on his list. The man she loved.

The future stretched ahead, uncertain but full of possibility. And for the first time since arriving at this ranch where Lucas had once spun his lies, Shannon felt hope outweighing fear.

———

PARKER'S GAZE FOLLOWED Shannon until she disappeared around the corner of the house, her words still echoing in his chest like a bell that had been struck. *I love you.* She'd said it. Not in the heat of passion or the safety of darkness, but in broad daylight with snow falling outside and his mother watching from twenty feet away.

The certainty in her voice, the way she'd looked at him like he was the only man in the world who mattered. It had changed something fundamental inside him. For the first time in his life, Parker felt truly chosen. Not by default, not because Lucas wasn't available, but because Shannon had weighed her options and decided she wanted him.

He turned toward the barn office, snagging his thermos from the desk before heading toward the tack room. He unscrewed the cap as he approached. Steam rose from the black coffee inside, carrying the rich aroma that had sustained him through countless cold mornings. Hopefully, the heat would thaw some of Mom's icy glares.

Parker hesitated just inside the doorway, studying his mother. She looked older as she moved between the saddle racks, her movements jerky and sharp. The scent of leather and saddle soap filled the small space, familiar and comforting despite the tension radiating from her rigid shoulders.

"Thought you might want some coffee," he offered, holding out the thermos cap that doubled as a cup. "It's still hot."

Mom glanced at the offering without slowing her movements. She was reorganizing bridles that didn't need reorganizing, her hands constantly moving.

"Don't need coffee," she muttered, lifting a bridle from

its hook only to hang it in the exact same spot. "Need to understand what that girl is really doing here."

Parker's jaw tightened, but he kept his voice level. "Shannon's here because she cares about me. She wants to help."

Mom let out a short, harsh laugh. "Shannon's here because she's playing house. Getting her closure, working through whatever unfinished business she has with Lucas by using you as a stand-in."

The words hit like a physical slap, but Parker forced himself to stay calm. He'd expected this. Had known his mother would twist Shannon's presence into something ugly and manipulative.

"That's not what this is," he whispered, setting the thermos on the wooden workbench. "You heard what she said out there. She loves me."

Mom's laugh came out harsh and cold. "Oh, she said the words, all right. Question is whether she means them for you or for the man she couldn't save."

She yanked another bridle from its peg, leather slapping against leather as she shook it out. The sound was sharp in the confined space, echoing off the walls lined with decades of accumulated tack.

"Mom—"

"You think you're the first man a woman's tried to fix?" Mom's voice climbed higher, her hands jerking at the bridle she was holding. "You think you're special because she picked you after Lucas broke her heart?"

Parker's hands curled into fists. "Shannon isn't trying to fix anyone."

"Isn't she?" Mom spun to face him, her gray eyes sharp and hard. "She dated your brother for six months, planned a future with him, and then what? Couldn't save him from himself, so now she thinks she can get it right with the good twin?"

The words hit like physical blows. His shoulders tensed,

every muscle going rigid.

"She's not—" he started, but his mother cut him off.

"She's using you, Parker. Maybe she doesn't even realize it, but that's what this is. You're her second chance, her do-over, her chance to prove she can love a Quaid man and make it work." Mom's voice rang with absolute conviction. "What happens when she gets what she needs? When she's worked through all that guilt and regret about Lucas? You think she'll still want the consolation prize?"

His chest tightened. Air refused to fill his lungs properly. Because wasn't that exactly what he was? The safe choice. The reliable alternative. The twin who wouldn't break her heart because he didn't have whatever it took to capture it completely.

"She's not using me." The words came out weaker than he intended.

"Poor boy." Mom's tone shifted, softened. "You always were too trusting for your own good. Too willing to see the best in people even when they didn't deserve it."

She turned back to the bridles, her movements slower now, almost gentle.

"Lucas has his faults, Lord knows, but at least he never pretends to be something he isn't. At least when he loves someone, it's honest."

Heat flooded through him—white-hot and blinding. His jaw clenched so hard his teeth ached. Every careful word he'd planned, every measured response, every attempt to be reasonable—gone.

"Honest?" The word tore out of him loud enough to echo off the walls. Mom's hands froze on the leather. "You think Lucas is honest? He lies about everything, Mom. Everything. Including how he felt about Shannon."

"Lucas loved that girl—"

"Lucas used her!" His voice cracked like a gunshot. "He manipulated her, stole from her, and destroyed her ability to trust anyone. That's not love. That's selfishness."

Mom turned slowly. Her eyes widened, her mouth opening slightly.

He'd never done this. Never pushed back. Never challenged the story she'd built around Lucas. His pulse hammered in his ears, but he didn't stop.

"And you know what the real tragedy is?" His voice shook, but he forced the words out anyway. "Shannon could see the difference between us in a few days. Days, Mom. But you? You've had thirty years, and you still think Lucas is the one worth fighting for."

"Parker—"

"You always loved him more, anyway." The words tore from his throat like they'd been ripped from some deep, infected wound. "The charming one, the exciting one, the one who needed saving. I was just the reliable backup plan, the son you could count on to clean up whatever mess Lucas made next."

Mom stared at him with wide, shocked eyes, her face pale in the dim light filtering through the tack room's single window. The bridle she'd been holding slipped from nerveless fingers to hit the concrete floor with a muffled thud.

"That's not—" she whispered, then stopped, her throat working soundlessly.

"It is true," Parker said, the rage draining out of him as quickly as it had come, leaving behind only exhaustion and the raw ache of finally speaking a truth he'd carried for too long. "Lucas was your favorite, and we both know it. He got your worry, your attention, your desperate hope that always painted the tiniest good deed into something praiseworthy. I got taken for granted because I was never the one falling apart."

His mother's face crumpled slightly, and for the first time, Parker saw her not as the formidable woman who'd shaped his childhood, but as someone broken by loss and blinded by her own grief.

"I never meant—" she started, then stopped again, her

hands trembling as she gripped the edge of the saddle rack.

"I know you didn't mean it," Parker said, his voice gentler now. "But that doesn't make it hurt less. And it doesn't give you the right to undermine the first good thing that's happened to me in years just because you can't stand the thought of Lucas being the villain in someone else's story."

The words hung between them in the leather-scented air, heavy with years of unspoken resentment and love turned toxic by grief. Parker could hear his own heartbeat in his ears, could smell the sharp scent of snow drifting through the cracked door, could feel the weight of everything that had just been broken open between them.

His mother stood frozen beside the saddle rack, her weathered hands gripping the wood hard enough to turn her knuckles white. The silence stretched between them, filled with the harsh truth of everything they'd never said to each other and the terrible clarity of everything they finally had.

Mom slowly released her grip on the saddle rack, her fingers trembling as she lowered them to her sides. She stared at Parker as if seeing him clearly for the first time in decades, her gray eyes widening.

"Oh, my boy," she whispered, the words barely audible in the quiet tack room. "What have I done?"

His mother's face cycled through emotions he'd rarely seen her display—shock, recognition, and something that might have been shame. She moved slowly, unsteadily, and sank onto the wooden bench that ran along the far wall.

"You were the easy one to love," she said finally, her voice thick and her eyes reddening. "That's what I told myself. Lucas needed so much—so much attention, so much fixing, so much hope—and you..." She looked up at him with eyes that suddenly seemed older than her years. "You were steady. Kind. You just quietly became everything a mother could want in a son, and I took that for granted."

Parker felt his throat close as she continued, each word

rippling through everything he'd believed about his place in their family.

"I didn't favor Lucas because I loved him more," Mom said, her hands clasped tightly in her lap. "I favored him because I was terrified of losing him completely. Every phone call, every arrest, every disappearance—I kept thinking this would be the one that took him away forever. So I poured everything I had into trying to save him."

She wiped her eyes with the back of her hand, a gesture so uncharacteristic it made Parker's chest ache.

"But you," she continued, meeting his gaze directly. "You were my safe harbor. The son I knew would always come home, would always do the right thing, would always be there when I needed him. I didn't worry about you because I didn't think I needed to. You were strong enough to take care of yourself."

"Mom—"

"Let me finish," she said, her voice gaining strength. "I see now how wrong I was. How much damage I did by always expecting you to be the strong one, the understanding one, the one who'd sacrifice his own needs for Lucas's latest crisis."

She stood slowly, moving toward the window where snow continued to fall in thick, lazy flakes. Her reflection in the glass looked fragile, breakable in a way Parker had never seen before.

"When Lucas brought Shannon here, I thought she was the answer. That she could fix him," Mom admitted. "A sweet, steady girl who could give him a reason to change, to settle down, to become the man I knew he could be if he just had the right motivation."

Parker's jaw tightened, but he remained silent, letting her work through whatever realization was dawning.

"When she left—when Lucas told me she'd broken things off because she didn't believe in him—I blamed her. I thought she'd given up too easily, hadn't loved him enough to see past his troubles." Mom's laugh was hollow, self-deprecating. "I never considered that maybe Lucas had hurt her so badly she had no choice but to protect herself."

She turned from the window, her eyes finding his again with startling clarity.

"But watching her these past few days, seeing the way she looks at you, the way she tries to help despite knowing I don't want her here..." Mom's voice softened. "That's not a woman trying to recapture something she lost. That's a woman who's found something she never expected to find."

Parker's heart hammered against his ribs as his mother continued, each word chipping away at the doubts she'd so carefully planted.

"She loves you, Parker. Not because you look like Lucas, but because you're everything he never was. Patient where he was impulsive. Honest where he was manipulative. Kind where he was selfish." Mom's smile was watery but genuine. "She loves you because you're you. And my grief blinded me from seeing that you deserve to be loved for exactly who you are."

The words hit Parker like warm sunlight after a long winter, melting something frozen deep inside his soul. For thirty years, he'd wondered if he was worthy of the same love his brother commanded so effortlessly. Now, his own mother was telling him he'd been worthy all along.

"I'm sorry," Mom said, her voice breaking slightly. "I'm so sorry for making you feel you were a second choice, like you weren't enough. You've always been enough, Parker. You've always been more than enough."

Parker crossed the small space between them in two quick strides, pulling his mother into a hug that felt like coming home after years of wandering. She felt smaller than he remembered, more fragile, but her arms around him were strong and sure.

"I love you, Mom," he whispered against her silver hair. "I always have."

"I love you too, son. More than you know." She pulled back to look at him, her eyes still bright with tears. "And I think it's time I stopped letting my fear of losing one son prevent me from celebrating the one I have."

They stood there for a moment, years of misunderstanding beginning to heal in the quiet sanctuary of the tack room. Outside, the snow continued to fall, muffling the world in peaceful silence.

"Maybe you could give an old woman a chance to make amends? To welcome the woman who loves her son the way he deserves to be loved."

Parker felt his throat tighten again, but this time it was with gratitude rather than pain. "I'd like that, Mom. So would Shannon."

Mom nodded, straightening her shoulders with visible effort. "Then let's go inside. I think I owe Shannon an apology. And maybe," she added with the first genuine smile he'd seen from her in days, "we can start figuring out how to be a family again."

They walked toward the house together, their footsteps crunching in harmony through the snow. And for the first time since arriving at Walnut Canyon Ranch, Parker felt like he was walking toward home rather than away from it.

15

SHANNON STOOD AT the kitchen counter, wrapping the leftover cornbread in aluminum foil while the morning light streamed through frost-etched windows. The scent of coffee and bacon still lingered in the air from the breakfast Joanna had insisted on making before their departure. Three days at Walnut Canyon Ranch had transformed from a dreaded ordeal into something approaching a family visit, complete with the comfortable rhythms of shared meals and easy conversation.

"You don't have to take that," Joanna said, drying her hands on the dish towel as she watched Shannon work. "It's just leftover cornbread."

"Are you kidding?" Shannon smiled, securing the foil edges. "This is the best cornbread I've ever had. Aunt Shirley's going to demand the recipe."

Joanna's cheeks flushed with pleased embarrassment. "It was my mother's recipe. Nothing fancy."

"The best recipes never are." Shannon tucked the wrapped bread into her overnight bag, alongside the jar of homemade strawberry preserves Joanna had pressed on her that morning. The gestures felt like peace offerings, small but meaningful bridges across the gap that had existed between them.

Parker appeared in the doorway, truck keys jingling in

his hand and a duffel bag slung over his shoulder. His hair was still damp from the shower, and he'd changed into his good jeans and a solid gray button-down shirt. Even dressed for the drive home, he looked relaxed in a way Shannon hadn't seen since they'd arrived.

"Ready?" he asked, but his attention was focused on his mother, who was hovering near the sink.

Shannon recognized the moment for what it was and stepped toward the living room. "I'll just grab my jacket and wait by the truck."

"Shannon." Joanna's voice stopped her at the threshold. "Thank you. For coming here, for helping with the ranch work, for being patient with a stubborn old woman who took too long to see what was right in front of her."

Shannon turned back to find Joanna's gray eyes bright with unshed tears, her weathered hands clasped tightly in front of her.

"Thank you for welcoming me into your home," she replied, meaning every word. "And for raising a man who'd give up everything to help his family."

"That's all Parker," Joanna said, glancing at her son with pride that had been missing from her voice three days ago. "I just finally stopped being too proud to appreciate what I had."

The conversation between mother and son that followed was quiet, intimate, conducted in the low tones of people working through years of accumulated hurt. Shannon gave them their privacy, stepping onto the porch where the morning air bit her cheeks and carried the clean scent of snow-covered pines.

The ranch looked different in the morning light. Less harsh, more welcoming. The pastures stretched toward the mountains that rose against a sky so blue it hurt to look at directly. She could understand why the Quaid family had built their lives here, despite the isolation and the endless work that came with caring for land and animals.

Fifteen minutes later, Parker emerged from the house, the lines around his eyes softer than she'd seen before. He hugged his mother on the porch, the embrace stretching longer than a simple goodbye. When they finally stepped apart, his mother cupped his face briefly, and he nodded at whatever she'd whispered.

"Drive carefully," Joanna called as they loaded their bags into the truck. "The roads can be tricky until you get past Flagstaff."

"We will," Parker promised, settling behind the wheel and adjusting the rearview mirror.

Shannon rolled down her window despite the cold. "Joanna? Would you like to come down for the New Year? I know Parker would love to show you Vargas Ranch, and Aunt Shirley would enjoy meeting you."

Joanna's eyebrows lifted, then her lips curved upward before pressing together. She glanced down at her hands, then back up. "I'd like that. Been a while since I went anywhere for fun instead of necessity. Brad should be back by then."

"Then it's settled," Shannon said, meaning it. "I'll call you with details once we get back."

The drive down the mountains began in comfortable silence, both of them processing the weekend that had changed so much between them. The truck's heater hummed steadily, fighting against the cold that pressed against the windows. Shannon watched the landscape change from snow-covered pines to high desert scrub, the elevation dropping with each mile that carried them away from Walnut Canyon Ranch.

"You've been quiet. Deep in thought or just vibing?" Parker asked when they'd been driving for nearly an hour, his voice gentle in the way that suggested he wasn't pushing, just offering space if she wanted to fill it.

Shannon shifted in her seat, angling her body toward him as much as the seatbelt would allow. "I was thinking about how wrong I was about your mother. And how right she was to be suspicious of me."

"What do you mean?"

"I mean, look at it from her perspective." She watched the desert roll past, dotted with scrub brush and cacti reaching toward the pale winter sky. "Her son brings home a woman who's supposedly going to save him from himself. Six months later, that woman is gone and Lucas is worse than ever. Then eight years pass, and suddenly the same woman shows up with the other twin."

Parker's hands tightened slightly on the steering wheel. "You're not the same woman who dated Lucas."

"No, but I look the same. Sound the same. Carry the same name." Shannon tucked a strand of hair behind her ear, remembering the shock on Joanna's face when she'd first recognized her. "If someone from my past showed up claiming to care about Aunt Shirley, I'd be suspicious too. Especially if that someone had history with a person who'd caused our family pain."

"Shannon." His voice carried a warning she didn't quite understand.

"I'm not defending what she said or how she treated me initially," she clarified quickly. "But I understand it now. She was protecting you the only way she knew how."

Parker was quiet for several miles, his attention focused on navigating the winding road. Shannon studied his profile, noting the tension that had crept back into his shoulders despite the successful resolution with his mother.

"What's bothering you?" she asked.

"Nothing. Everything went fine with Mom."

"Parker." She waited until he glanced at her before continuing. "We just spent three days learning that honesty works better than protective silence. Don't shut me out now."

A muscle in his jaw ticked, but he didn't respond immediately. The silence stretched until Shannon began to worry she'd pushed too hard, asked for more vulnerability than he was ready to share.

"What if she was right?" The words came out quietly, almost lost under the sound of the truck's engine. "Not about her reasons for being suspicious, but about her concerns. What if you are here because of some unfinished business with Lucas?"

Shannon felt like she'd been slapped. "You think I'm using you?"

"I think," Parker said carefully, his voice strained, "that you're the strongest, most genuine person I've ever met. But I also think Lucas hurt you in ways you're still discovering, and I wonder if being with me is part of how you're trying to heal from that."

"Pull over."

"Shannon —"

"Pull over, Parker. Now."

He found a scenic overlook about a mile down the road, the truck's tires crunching on gravel as he parked facing a view of the valley spread below them. The engine ticked as it cooled, the only sound besides the wind hissing through the vents.

Shannon unbuckled her seatbelt and turned to face him fully, her heart pounding with a mixture of hurt and fierce determination. "Do you remember what I told you in the barn yesterday morning?"

He nodded, his blue eyes wary. "You said you loved me."

"I said I loved you. Not that I was healing through you, not that I was working through trauma, not that I was trying to rewrite history." She reached for his hands, holding them between hers despite their chill. "I said I loved you, Parker Quaid, because of who you are, not because of who you're not."

"But you can't deny that Lucas —"

"Lucas hurt me," Shannon interrupted firmly. "He lied

to me, stole from me, made me question my ability to judge character or trust my own instincts. Those are facts, and I won't pretend they didn't happen or that they didn't affect me."

His shoulders sagged slightly, and she could see him bracing for whatever painful truth she was about to deliver.

"But Parker," she continued, her voice softening, "healing isn't about forgetting or pretending trauma never happened. Healing is about choosing wholeness despite the wounds. It's about recognizing that one person's betrayal doesn't define everyone else's character."

She shifted closer, close enough that she could feel the warmth of his breath against her cheek, close enough that her next words carried the weight of absolute certainty.

"I don't love you because you're helping me heal from Lucas. I love you because you would have emptied your savings to give me something I wanted. Because you dropped everything to drive two hours for your mom. Because you treat horses like family. Because you show up every day and do the right thing, even when it's hard or no one's watching."

Her voice grew stronger, more passionate, as she continued. "I love you because you're patient with Dylan's stutter and protective of Braden's dreams and respectful to your mother even when she's being impossible. I love you because you've been judged your whole life for someone else's choices, and instead of becoming bitter, you became kind."

Tears spilled over her lower lashes, but her gaze never wavered from his. "I love you, Parker, because you're exactly the man I didn't know I was looking for. Not the safe version of someone dangerous, not the consolation prize after someone better, not the rebound after someone worse. You're the prize. You're the answer to prayers I was afraid to pray."

Parker stared at her, his throat working as he processed her words. She could see the moment when belief began to overcome doubt, when her certainty started to dissolve the fears his mother's warnings had planted.

"I'm sorry," he whispered, lifting one hand to cup her cheek. "I didn't mean to doubt what we have. I just—"

"You've spent a lifetime having people see Lucas when they look at you," Shannon said, leaning into his touch. "Of course you'd worry that I might be doing the same thing. But Parker, I stopped seeing Lucas the day I watched you with Braden. Maybe even before that, when you showed me your scar and I realized identical didn't mean indistinguishable."

She covered his hand with hers, anchoring the contact between them. "You want to know the difference between you and Lucas? Lucas made me feel special because I was useful to him. You make me feel cherished because I'm me. Lucas saw what he could take from me. You see what you can give to me."

"Shannon." Her name was barely a breath, reverent and wondering.

"Lucas made promises he never intended to keep," she continued. "You make commitments you'd die before breaking. Lucas charmed me into trusting him. You earned my trust by being trustworthy, day after day, choice after choice."

The tears on her cheeks felt warm against the chilly air seeping through the truck's windows, but she didn't care about the cold or the discomfort or anything except making sure Parker understood the truth of what existed between them.

"I know the difference between healing and love," she said firmly. "Healing feels like letting go of weight you've carried too long. Love feels like finding something worth carrying forever. What I feel for you, Parker, is definitely the second thing."

He leaned forward, resting his forehead against hers, his eyes closed as if he was absorbing her words through more than just his hearing.

"I love you too," he whispered. "More than I thought I could love anyone. I'm sorry I let doubt creep in."

"Don't apologize for being human," Shannon said, her voice gentle now that the worst of the crisis had passed. "Just promise me that when fear tries to convince you I'm settling for second best, you'll remember this conversation. Remember that I had eight years to find someone else if I'd wanted to. Remember that I chose you, not because you were available, but because you're irreplaceable."

Parker's answer was a kiss, soft and sweet and full of promises that had nothing to do with words. When they broke apart, the tension that had been building between them had dissolved into something deeper, more solid, and peacefully honest.

Back on the road, Shannon settled into comfortable silence, watching the desert landscape roll past. The crisis had passed, and what remained felt stronger for having weathered the storm.

They reached her apartment complex as the afternoon shadows lengthened. Parker walked her to the door, his hand warm against the small of her back.

"I'll pick you up Christmas morning," he said. "Eight-thirty?"

"I'll be ready."

He cupped her face in both hands, his thumbs brushing her cheekbones as he studied her like he was memorizing every detail. Then he kissed her slowly and tenderly. She heard every unspoken word in that kiss so full of promise and joy.

When he pulled back, he smiled at her, that rare full smile that crinkled the corners of his eyes. He touched his fingers to the brim of his cowboy hat before climbing behind the wheel.

She watched from her doorway until his truck disappeared around the corner. Inside, she leaned against the closed door, her hand pressed to her lips where his kiss still lingered.

———

Parker stood outside Shannon's apartment building at eight-thirty Christmas morning, holding a travel mug of coffee and fighting the grin that had been threatening to split his face since he'd woken up. Seventy-degree weather and clear skies were perfect for the long drive downtown. More importantly, it meant courtside seats to watch their beloved Phoenix Suns take on the Lakers on Christmas Day.

They were about to live a dream they'd both carried since childhood.

Shannon appeared at her door in dark jeans and a vintage Suns t-shirt that looked like it had been loved through multiple seasons, her hair pulled back in a ponytail and her face bright with excitement that matched his own.

"Ready?" she asked, locking the door behind her with hands that trembled slightly.

"Are you nervous?" Parker asked, noting the tremor as he helped her into the truck.

"Nervous? I'm terrified." Shannon buckled her seatbelt, then turned to face him with eyes that sparkled with anticipation. "What if I embarrass myself? What if I spill something on you?"

"Then I'll have the most unique shirt in the arena." He reached across the console to take her hand. "Shannon, breathe. We're going to have the time of our lives."

She squeezed his hand, then shifted in her seat, the movement drawing his attention. "Speaking of being together more..." She paused, and he could see her gathering courage. "What would you think if I moved closer to Wickenburg? Not all the way to the ranch, just... cut the commute in half."

Parker's heart kicked against his ribs. "It'd make the

drive easier."

Her eyes searched his face. "That's not really what I'm asking."

He knew exactly what she was asking. Ever since their trip to his mother's place—since that overlook where she declared her love with a fierceness that still made his chest expand—he'd been thinking about this. About how much he wanted to just show up at her door with takeout after a long day. About stopping by on his way home from town instead of calculating whether he had time for a three-hour round trip. About what it would mean to have her close enough that "see you soon" didn't require planning days in advance.

"I mean," she continued when he didn't respond right away, "would you want me closer? Not rushing anything. Just... near enough to be part of the rhythm. Regular dates that don't require half a tank of gas..."

"Yes." The word came out rougher than he intended. He cleared his throat. "Shannon, I've been wanting to ask you the same thing but didn't know if it was too soon. An hour and fifteen minutes each way means we're spending half our time in vehicles."

Her smile started slow, then bloomed into something that made his pulse jump. "So you'd want me closer."

"I want you close enough that I can bring you dinner when you've had a long day. Close enough that 'see you tonight' doesn't mean I need to leave work by three." He glanced at her, then back at the road. "Close enough that this doesn't feel like we're always saying goodbye."

"Good. I've been month-to-month for a while now. I'll start looking for a place in Wickenburg."

They filled the drive with an animated discussion about the team, Shannon's encyclopedic knowledge amazed him. Parker stole glances at her profile as she talked—the way her eyes lit up, the way her hands moved to emphasize a point.

"Courtside, center court, home side," Parker said, shaking his head. "Close enough to hear the players talking to each other."

"Close enough to see if the forward really does complain about every call," Shannon added with a grin that made Parker's heart skip.

The arena rose before them like a temple to basketball, its modern architecture gleaming in the desert sun. He found a parking spot, his hands steady despite the adrenaline coursing through his system. Years of following this team, of watching games on television, of dreaming about moments exactly like this one.

"Parker." Shannon's voice was soft, understanding. "Take a minute. Just breathe this in."

He looked at her sitting beside him in the truck, surrounded by the sounds of fans and distant music from the arena, and felt something settle deeply. She was right. This was a moment worth savoring.

"Dad would have loved this," Parker said. "Seeing us sitting courtside, watching the team we all followed together. He always said the Suns have the most loyal fans in the league."

"He was right about that," Shannon said, her voice soft with understanding. "And he sees you now. He knows you're exactly where you're supposed to be, with exactly the right person."

Parker lifted their joined hands to his lips, pressing a soft kiss to her knuckles. "Thank you. For being here, for understanding what this means to both of us, for making sure we don't take a single moment for granted."

"Thank you," she replied, "for seeing this as ours instead of yours. For letting me back into something I thought I'd lost forever."

The arena concourse buzzed with holiday energy as Parker presented their tickets to the courtside attendant. The walk through the tunnel toward the court felt like stepping into another dimension, and then suddenly they emerged into the arena proper.

Parker stopped breathing.

The court stretched before them, polished wood gleaming under bright lights, surrounded by twenty thousand empty seats that would soon hold screaming fans.

"Oh my," Shannon breathed beside him, her voice filled with wonder.

Their seats were perfect, close enough that Parker could see every detail.

"Look around." Shannon already had her phone out. "I want you to remember every detail."

His gaze traveled across the arena as it filled with waves of orange and purple. When the players emerged for warm-ups, Parker's pulse kicked up. Everything he'd only watched from his living room was happening fifteen feet away.

The national anthem played as twenty thousand people stood with hands over hearts. Parker felt tears prick his eyes as he looked around at the sea of faces, all united in their love for this game, this team, this moment.

When they announced the starting lineups, Parker launched to his feet, shouting along with everyone else. Shannon laughed beside him, clutching his arm.

The opening tip sent both teams into motion, and Parker understood immediately why television couldn't capture this. The speed was breathtaking; the sound of every collision visceral.

"They're so much faster than I expected," he said during the first timeout.

"This is everything I hoped it would be," Shannon said, eyes radiant. "Being here with you, watching our team, living this dream together."

Parker watched her face several times during the first half. The way she leaned forward during crucial possessions, the way she grabbed his arm during tense moments, the way her whole body moved with every play. This was the Shannon his brother had tried to destroy. And she was here with him — laughing, cheering, completely present.

At halftime, the Suns held a six-point lead.

"I keep expecting to wake up," Shannon admitted. "Eight years since I've been to a game, and now we're here, courtside, on Christmas Day."

"It's real," Parker assured her, reaching over to squeeze her hand.

The second half brought even more intensity. With three minutes remaining and the Suns clinging to a two-point lead, a loose ball bounced directly toward their section. Both Shannon and Parker instinctively reached out, their fingers brushing the leather as a Lakers player dove to retrieve it, landing just inches from their feet.

"We just touched a game ball!" Shannon exclaimed, her eyes wide with amazement.

"Together," Parker replied, staring at their hands like they'd been blessed.

The final minutes were torture and ecstasy combined. Shannon had grabbed nachos during the previous timeout, the cardboard tray balanced precariously in her lap as both of them leaned forward, completely absorbed.

With forty seconds remaining and the game tied, a shooting guard got the ball at the top of the key. Shannon grabbed Parker's arm with her free hand as the clock wound down. "This is it," she breathed.

He drove hard, pulled up, and released a perfect jump shot. As the ball swished through the net, both Shannon and Parker exploded to their feet. In her excitement, Shannon's nachos went flying, cheese and chips scattering across Parker's chest and shoulder.

"Oh, no!" she gasped, her hands flying to her mouth in horror. "I'm so sorry, I—"

But Parker was laughing, pure joy radiating through him as he looked at her—cheese sauce on her fingers, mortification in her eyes, her Suns t-shirt slightly askew from jumping up. Without hesitation, he cupped her face in his hands and kissed her, right there courtside, with twenty thousand people screaming around them.

The arena cameras caught it immediately. Their kiss appeared on the jumbotron, and the crowd's roar somehow got even louder. When they finally broke apart, both laughing, the entire arena was cheering for them.

"We're on the big screen!" Shannon laughed, pointing up at their image.

"I don't care," Parker said, brushing a chip crumb from her hair. "You can spill nachos on me at every game for the rest of our lives."

The Suns held on to win, but the final score mattered less than the perfect moment they'd created together. As confetti fell from the rafters, Parker and Shannon held each other close, both of them glowing with shared euphoria.

"So?" Parker asked, watching Shannon's face. "Did it live up to years of dreaming?"

"It exceeded them," she said, her voice still hoarse from cheering. "I've missed this so much—the energy, the passion, the way the game feels from this close. But sharing it with you?" Her smile was radiant. "That made it perfect."

They remained in their seats as the arena gradually emptied, neither wanting to end the magical afternoon.

"We should probably start heading home," Shannon said reluctantly. "But I need to say something first."

Parker turned to face her. Her smile had faded, though her eyes still held that earlier brightness.

"When I was in college, when I had season tickets with Aunt Shirley, I used to dream about sharing games like this with someone who loved basketball as much as I did." She reached for his hands, still slightly sticky from the nacho incident. "I gave up that dream when I lost the tickets. But sitting here with you, living this together—it's better than anything I ever imagined back then."

The words hit him square in the chest. She'd just told him he'd given back something Lucas had stolen.

"Shannon." His voice came out rougher than he intended. He cleared his throat, tried again. "When you jumped up and sent those nachos flying—" A laugh escaped him, helpless against the emotion building in his throat. "I wasn't thinking about the game anymore. I was just... you were so happy."

He squeezed her hands, not trusting himself with more words.

"Good," she said, her smile brilliant even with cheese still smudged on her chin. "Because I loved every second of it. The basketball, the atmosphere, spilling food on you like a complete amateur, getting caught kissing on the jumbotron—all of it. This was perfect."

"That last part was my favorite," Parker said, his grin spreading wide.

She nudged his shoulder with a laugh. "Of course it was."

They walked back to the truck slower than they'd come, neither one ready for the day to end.

"I'm never going to forget this," Shannon said as they pulled out of the parking structure. "Not a single detail."

"Me neither." Parker glanced at her, then back at the road.

"Thank you," Shannon said quietly as they reached her apartment complex, the same words she'd said that morning but weighted now with the gravity of everything they'd shared.

"Thank you. This was the best day of my life," Parker replied, leaning across the console to kiss her softly, tasting the lingering salt from the nachos and not caring one bit.

And it had been the best day of his life. Not just because of courtside seats or watching the Suns win on Christmas Day. Because he'd watched Shannon light up during every play, heard her laugh when that loose ball came their way, felt her grab his arm during every tense moment. The woman who'd once called the sheriff on him had become the woman who made his biggest dreams come true. And tomorrow, whatever challenges arose, they'd face them together.

16

PARKER SAT IN the hard plastic chair in the county jail's waiting room, his hands clasped tightly between his knees as he stared at the institutional pale gray walls. The smell of disinfectant hung in the air, mixing with the distant sounds of conversations in multiple languages and the intermittent buzz of security doors opening and closing.

Three days had passed since Christmas. Since courtside seats and Shannon's laughter and that kiss on the jumbotron. Three days since he had dropped her off at her place with another lingering kiss that had made him want to never leave her side. He'd replayed every moment of that date a hundred times, holding onto the warmth of it like a talisman.

But today wasn't about joy or new beginnings. Today was about facing the past.

This time he wasn't at the jail because he'd been mistaken for his twin. This time, Lucas was the one behind bars.

Mom had called later that night on his way back to the ranch with the news that they'd finally arrested Lucas and were holding him at the Maricopa County Jail. So, he and Mom had decided to visit him this morning before heading over to Shannon's Aunt Shirley's for a belated Christmas meal.

A passage from Ephesians kept echoing in his mind: *Be*

kind and compassionate to one another, forgiving one another, just as God also forgave you in Christ. Adan had pointed out that forgiveness wasn't about the other person's response. It was about releasing the burden of bitterness and choosing to extend the same grace God had shown him.

Ever since that Bible study with Adan, Parker couldn't shake the conviction that God was asking him to forgive Lucas. Not because his twin deserved it but because God had forgiven Parker and given him a new life in Christ. A life he didn't deserve either.

And now here he was. Seconds away from the moment where he would put that conviction into practice.

A guard appeared in the doorway and called their names. Parker helped his mother to her feet, feeling the tremor in her hand as she gripped his arm. They followed the guard through a series of security doors, each one closing behind them with a metallic clang that seemed to seal them further from the world of hope and second chances.

The visitation room was small and sterile, divided by thick plexiglass. Lucas sat on the other side, dressed in an orange jumpsuit that didn't diminish his confident posture. His hair was uncombed, his jaw shadowed with stubble, but his eyes held the same calculating chill they'd always carried.

Parker picked up the phone on their side of the glass, his mother leaning close to hear. Lucas did the same, with a slight smile playing at the corners of his mouth.

"Hey, twin," Lucas said, as casually as if they were meeting for coffee. "Didn't expect to see you here."

"Lucas." Parker took a steadying breath, feeling his mother's hand tighten on his arm. "I came because I needed to tell you something."

"Let me guess." Lucas leaned back in his chair, utterly relaxed. "You're disappointed in me? You think I should feel bad about what I did? Save the sermon, Parker. I've heard it all before."

"I forgive you."

The words hung in the air between them, and for just a moment, Lucas's mask of casual indifference slipped. Just for a beat. Then it was back, stronger than before, accompanied by a bitter laugh.

"You forgive me?" Lucas repeated, his tone mocking. "For what, exactly? For being smarter than the marks I con? For not settling for your boring, ordinary life?"

"For everything," Parker said calmly. "For using my name and my social, for the crimes you committed that put my reputation and livelihood at risk, and for the pain you've caused Mom. For years of lies and manipulation."

And for hurting Shannon. That was the hardest to forgive. He'd let Lucas discover some other time that Parker intended to make a life with the wonderful woman his twin stole from.

"How generous of you." Lucas's smile turned sharp. "Must feel good, being the better twin. The one who stayed home. Who plays by the rules. Who gets to be the hero."

Mom flinched beside him, but he kept his focus on his brother's face. "I'm not forgiving you because I'm better than you, Lucas. I'm forgiving you because God forgave me when I didn't deserve it. Because holding onto anger and bitterness was eating me alive. I'm choosing to let it go."

"How noble." Lucas glanced at their mother, his expression shifting to something almost tender. "Don't worry, Mom. I'll be out of here soon. My lawyer says the evidence is circumstantial, and the lady in Scottsdale can't positively identify—"

"Lucas, stop." Their mother's voice cut through his words, stronger than Parker had heard it in years. "Just stop."

Lucas's eyebrows rose. "Mom?"

"I came here hoping..." She paused, pressing her free hand against the plexiglass as if she could reach through it. "I've spent years hoping you'd change. Making excuses, believing that somewhere inside you was the boy I raised, the son who just needed the right motivation or the right support to become the man I knew you could be."

"And now?" Lucas asked, his tone carefully neutral.

"Now I see you clearly," she said, and Parker heard the tears in her voice even as her words remained steady. "You're not a troubled son who needs help. You're a man who likes who he is. Who likes hurting people. And no amount of love or prayer or second chances is going to change that, because you don't want to change."

For the first time since they'd sat down, Lucas's expression went completely blank. Not angry, not defensive, just... empty.

Then he narrowed his eyes and lifted his chin.

"You're right," he said finally. "I don't want to change. This is who I am, Mom. This is who I've always been. You just didn't want to see it."

Parker watched his mother's face crumple, watched years of hope die in her eyes. He wanted to rage at Lucas, to demand he show some remorse, some recognition of the pain he was causing. But he'd come here to offer forgiveness, and forgiveness meant releasing Lucas to face the consequences of his own choices.

"I'll keep praying for you anyway," Parker said, surprised by the steadiness in his own voice. "Not because I expect you to change on my timeline, or even in my lifetime. But I have to believe God can reach your heart. His grace is bigger than your choices."

Lucas studied him for a long moment, something unreadable flickering across his face. Then he shrugged and stood up. "Well, this has been touching. Thanks for the visit."

He hung up the phone without waiting for a response and turned away, signaling to the guard that he was ready to go back to his cell. Parker watched his twin's back disappear through the security door, a weight settling onto his shoulders one last time before finally, mercifully, it began to lift.

The security door buzzed open, and they emerged into the waiting room, his mother shaking at his side. He slung his arm around her shoulders.

"I'm sorry, Mom," he whispered against her silver hair. "I know how much you wanted to believe he could change."

"He doesn't want to change," she said, her voice muffled against his shoulder. "He likes who he is. He likes hurting people."

Parker held her while she cried. The stark honesty of Lucas's admission had been brutal, but it had also been freeing. No more wondering, no more hoping for something that would never come.

"But you did the right thing in there," Mom said, pulling back to look at him with wonder in her grief-stricken eyes. "Forgiving him like that. Even when he threw it back in your face."

"Thanks, Mom," Parker said.

She stared at him as if seeing him clearly for the first time. "When did you become so wise?"

"When I finally stopped trying to carry burdens that were never mine to bear," he replied, leading her toward the exit. "Lucas makes his own choices, Mom. His failures don't reflect on us, and his crimes aren't our responsibility to fix."

They stepped out into the warm Arizona sun, a stark contrast to the institutional coldness they'd left behind. Parker helped his mother into the truck, noting the way her hands shook slightly as she buckled her seatbelt.

"Are you okay?" he asked, settling behind the wheel but making no move to start the engine.

"I think so," she said slowly, as if testing the words for truth. "It hurts seeing him like that. Hearing him admit he doesn't want to change. But I am at peace with it."

Parker nodded, understanding exactly what she meant.

"I have something else to tell you," his mother said as he

started the truck and pulled out of the parking lot. "Something I should have mentioned earlier, but I wanted to wait until after we saw Lucas."

"What's that?"

"All that money you've been sending me for the past three years? I've been saving it."

His hands tightened on the steering wheel. "Saving it?"

"Every penny," she confirmed, her voice growing stronger. "The life insurance from your father's policy covered the mortgage, and I've been managing okay on what the land produces. But I knew you needed to send it, needed to feel you were helping, so I let you."

Parker's brow furrowed.

"I've been saving it because I knew that someday, you'd need it to build your own life," she continued, reaching into her purse to pull out an envelope. "And that day has come."

She handed him the envelope at the next red light. The thickness surprised him. Every penny he'd scraped together since Dad passed away and she'd saved his money for him.

He swallowed past the lump in his throat. "Mom—"

"It's enough money to put a down payment on your own place," she said, tears beginning to track down her cheeks. "And I signed a contract with Brad Riggs to hire him as the full-time ranch manager for Walnut Canyon."

Parker stared at the envelope as if it might explode in his hands. "You don't want me to come home?"

"I'm giving you permission to build the life you want," she corrected gently. "With the woman you love, in the place where you've found happiness. You don't owe me your whole life just because Lucas threw his away."

The traffic light turned green, but Parker sat frozen, unable to process the magnitude of what his mother was offering. Freedom. Financial security. The chance to build something with Shannon without the constant weight of family obligation pulling him in another direction.

"Parker, honey, you need to drive." Mom patted his

arm.

He eased forward through the intersection, his mind reeling. "I can't take this. It's too much."

"It's exactly the right amount," she replied firmly. "Your father always said the best gift parents could give their children was the tools to build their own happiness. This is my gift to you, and to Shannon, and to whatever beautiful life you're going to create together."

They drove in silence for several miles, the envelope sitting between them like a bridge between his past and his future. Outside the truck windows, the desert landscape rolled past. Saguaro cacti stood proudly against the pale sky, with the mountains rising in the distance.

"Why now?" Parker finally asked. "Why today?"

"Because I watched you in there," his mother replied. "Watched you offer forgiveness to someone who didn't want it, didn't deserve it, and threw it back in your face. You did it anyway because it was the right thing to do. Because God forgave you."

Her voice broke slightly on the last words, and Parker had to blink hard to keep his vision clear.

"That's who you are, Parker," she continued. "A man who stays, who cares, and who loves with a generosity that makes everything around him more beautiful. Your father would be so proud if he could see you now."

Parker coughed and pinched the bridge of his nose for a few seconds. Then he turned on the radio, Christmas songs filling the cab even though it was New Year's Eve.

As they approached Wickenburg, the familiar landmarks of his new life came into view. The desert that had become his home, the community that had embraced him, and the woman who'd taught him what it meant to be chosen for exactly who he was.

"Shannon's special," Parker said.

"She's perfect for you," Mom agreed. "And you're perfect for her. I was too proud and too scared to see it at first, but watching you two together made it impossible to deny. You make each other better. You bring out the best in each other."

Parker turned onto the road leading to Aunt Shirley's house, the elegant stucco structure coming into view between the palo verde trees. Warm light spilled from the windows, and he could see figures moving around inside. Shannon and her great-aunt prepared for their week-late Christmas celebration.

He pulled into the circular drive and cut the engine, but didn't immediately reach for the door handle. The weight of everything that had happened—offering forgiveness to Lucas, watching his mother finally see her sons clearly, receiving her blessing to build his own life—it all pressed against his chest like something physical. Welcoming. Freeing.

Parker took a slow breath, his hands still gripping the steering wheel. The house ahead represented everything he'd been afraid to hope for. Inside waited the woman he loved, preparing a meal that would bring their unconventional family together. His mother sat beside him, finally free from the burden of trying to save someone who didn't want to be saved. And in his pocket rested an envelope that made a future with Shannon even more possible.

He glanced at his mom, who was watching him with patient understanding.

"Ready?" she asked softly.

Parker nodded, releasing the steering wheel. "Yeah. I'm ready."

They walked toward the house together, and Parker marveled at the quiet joy of coming home to people who saw him exactly as he was and loved him anyway.

17

SHANNON STIRRED THE gravy with one hand while reaching for the salt with the other, the rich aroma of roasting turkey filling Aunt Shirley's spacious kitchen. Through the window above the sink, she could see the desert landscape painted in the soft gold of late afternoon, December thirty-first stretching toward evening with the promise of a new year just hours away.

"That smells like heaven," Aunt Shirley said, emerging from the dining room where she'd been setting the table with her good china.

"I hope it tastes as good as it smells," Shannon replied, checking the turkey's temperature one more time. "I'm a little nervous about cooking a holiday meal for Joanna."

"Nonsense. You're a wonderful cook, and besides, this isn't about impressing anyone." Aunt Shirley adjusted the arrangement of winter roses in the crystal vase she'd placed on the counter. "This is about celebrating family."

Warmth bloomed in her chest at the word family. Six months ago, her family had included Aunt Shirley, her father, and the professional relationships she'd built through her great-aunt's nonprofit. Now it included Parker, Joanna, and the entire Vargas Ranch community that had welcomed her with open arms.

"I still can't believe how much has changed since that

first day at the ranch," Shannon said, her mind drifting back to the mortifying moment when she had called the sheriff on the man who would become the center of her world. "If someone had told me then I'd be hosting Parker's mother for our deferred Christmas celebration, I would have laughed."

"Would you?" Aunt Shirley's tone carried the subtle amusement of someone who'd seen more of life's ironies than most. "I seem to remember you calling me a few weeks later, asking many questions about identical twins and whether people could really change."

Heat crept up Shannon's neck as she remembered that conversation. The confusion, the fear, the desperate need to understand how someone could look exactly like her ex but feel completely different. "I was so scared I was making the same mistake again."

"And what do you think now?"

Shannon set down the wooden spoon, considering the question seriously. "I think Parker is exactly who he's always been. Kind, steady, and genuine. Lucas's choices never had the power to change that, but it took me a while to see it clearly."

"And Lucas?"

The question hung in the air between them, weighted with everything Shannon had been processing since Joanna's phone call three days ago. They'd finally arrested Lucas in Scottsdale after he had run another con under a false name. According to Joanna, there was a victim—another widow he'd manipulated—but Shannon didn't know the details. And she didn't need to.

"I forgive him," Shannon said, surprising herself with the certainty in her voice. "Not because he deserves it, and not because what he did was okay. But because carrying that bitterness was hurting me."

Aunt Shirley's expression softened with approval and something that looked like pride. "That's real growth, sweetheart. Born out of wrestling with hard truths and choosing forgiveness."

Shannon nodded, letting the truth of those words settle deep in her bones. The forgiveness hadn't come easily or all at once. It had been a gradual process of recognizing that her healing didn't depend on Lucas facing consequences, but on her willingness to release the bitterness that had kept her heart partially closed for years.

"What really amazes me is how Parker handled everything when Joanna called with the news," Shannon said, pulling the turkey from the oven and setting it on the cooling rack. "He didn't hesitate when she asked him to visit Lucas. Just said yes."

"That tells you something about the man's character."

"It tells me everything." Shannon transferred the turkey to a cutting board. "He showed up for his mother, even knowing how hard it would be."

They worked in comfortable silence for a few minutes, the kitchen filling with the sounds of a meal coming together — the clink of serving spoons against ceramic, the soft pop of lids being removed from covered dishes.

"Speaking of Parker," Aunt Shirley said as she arranged dinner rolls in a basket, "I've been thinking about your living situation."

Shannon raised an eyebrow. "My living situation?"

"That commute from Phoenix is wearing you down, honey. An hour and fifteen minutes each way, sometimes more with traffic. I know you want to be closer." Aunt Shirley pulled a dish towel from the drawer, her movements casual despite the weight of what she was suggesting. "This house has six bedrooms, and I'm rattling around in it like a marble in a mason jar. You could have the entire east wing if you wanted privacy. Your own entrance, your own space, but close enough to Vargas Ranch that you could spend more time with that cowboy of yours."

Shannon looked up from the mashed potatoes, her throat tight. She and Parker had talked about the future, but hearing someone else say it out loud felt different. Real.

"And besides," Aunt Shirley added with a knowing smile, "something tells me you won't need your own place for too much longer, anyway."

Heat rose in Shannon's cheeks. "Aunt Shirley—"

"What? Am I wrong?"

Shannon busied herself with the mashed potatoes, her hands not quite steady. "We've only known each other for a few months. Do you think we're ready for marriage? It feels like a big step."

"Ready?" Aunt Shirley set down the dish towel and turned to face her directly. "Honey, there's no magic time-line that works for every couple. Your uncle Henry and I knew after three weeks. My parents courted for two years. Both marriages lasted until death parted us." She reached out and squeezed Shannon's hand. "If you're both seeking God in all things, let Him lead you to the timing that's right for you two. Not what some books say, not what your friends did, not what feels 'normal.' Just what's right be-tween you and Parker and the Lord."

The words settled over Shannon like a blessing. She thought about the way Parker prayed with her, the way they talked through decisions together, the way their faith had become intertwined with their relationship. Maybe that was the real measure not months on a calendar.

"Thank you," Shannon whispered.

"Now, about the east wing—"

The sound of tires on gravel announced Parker and Jo-anna's return from the Maricopa County Jail. Shannon's pulse quickened with anticipation and concern, wondering how the visit with Lucas had gone, whether Joanna was okay, and whether Parker had found any peace in the en-counter.

She'd been working through her own feelings about Lu-cas all afternoon—praying, processing, trying to understand the tangled mess of anger and pity and relief that came with knowing he was finally facing consequences. She'd realized something important in those quiet hours: forgiving Lucas wasn't about him at all. It was about choosing freedom for herself, about refusing to let his past crimes steal her present joy.

"They're back," she said unnecessarily, moving toward the window to glimpse Parker's truck pulling up the circular drive.

"Let them come to us," Aunt Shirley suggested gently. "Give them a moment to process what happened before we bombard them with questions."

Shannon nodded, though every instinct urged her to run outside and wrap Parker in her arms. The visit to the county jail couldn't have been easy for either of them.

She busied herself with final meal preparations, arranging serving spoons and checking that everything was ready to transfer to the dining room. The turkey rested on the cutting board, waiting to be sliced. The gravy was smooth and rich. The vegetables were tender but not overcooked. Everything was ready for their postponed Christmas celebration, their chance to come together as a family despite the difficult circumstances that had brought them to this moment.

The front door opened, followed by a soft thud of boots being removed in the entryway, and Shannon's heart lifted at the sound. Whatever they'd faced at the jail, Parker was here now. They were together, and that was what mattered most.

Soon they would sit around Aunt Shirley's beautiful table, sharing a meal that represented new beginnings and hard-won peace. Soon Shannon would tell Parker about her decision to move to Wickenburg, to root herself completely in this life they were building together.

But first, she would hold him, and let him know that whatever he'd faced today, he hadn't faced it alone. He never would again.

———

As SOON AS Parker entered and toed off his boots, Shannon appeared in a forest green sweater that made her brown hair shine in the foyer light. The sight of her calmed him after the emotional gauntlet of the jail visit. Sitting across from Lucas in that sterile room, he'd held onto the thought of coming back here to her.

Her eyes immediately sought his, searching his face.

"How are you?" she asked softly, moving closer.

Parker reached for her hand, needing the contact. "Better now." He meant it completely. The weight he'd carried into that jail had lifted somewhere between watching his mother finally see Lucas clearly and walking back out into the Arizona sunlight knowing he was free. Free from guilt that had never been his to carry. Free from the burden of trying to fix what Lucas had broken.

He handed her the envelope as they moved into the great room. "Mom saved all the money I'd been sending. For us."

"Wait, what?"

Parker pulled her closer into a brief embrace, pressing a kiss to her temple. "You heard me. For us."

When he released her, he noticed the pink on her cheeks and that soft smile he'd grown to love stretching across her lips.

"How are your turkey-carving skills?"

Parker laughed. "Dad made sure I could wield an electric knife safely."

The next hour passed in a blur of conversation. Mom processed the visit with Lucas. Parker told Shannon about forgiving his brother.

As they ate too much turkey and stuffing, they told stories about holidays past. Parker watched the interplay between the three women who'd become the center of his world. His mother, finally free from the burden of trying to save someone who didn't want to be saved. Shannon, glowing with the quiet happiness of someone who'd found her place in the world. Aunt Shirley, presiding over it all with the satisfaction of someone who'd helped orchestrate a perfect ending to the year.

"This is the best Christmas I've had in years," his mother said as they finished the main course, her voice thick with emotion. "Thank you for including me in your family."

"Thank you for letting us be your family," Shannon replied, reaching across the table to squeeze Joanna's hand.

When the meal ended and they moved to the living room for coffee and dessert, Parker sat on the loveseat beside Shannon, her head resting against his shoulder while Aunt Shirley regaled them with stories from her days as a voice coach to Hollywood stars. The fireplace crackled softly, casting shadows on the walls, and outside the windows, the desert night sky stretched endlessly overhead.

"I should probably head back to the guest cottage," his mother said as the grandfather clock in the hallway chimed ten o'clock. "It's been a long day, and I want to give you young people some time together."

"I'll drive you," Parker offered, but Aunt Shirley waved him back down.

"Nonsense. I'll take her myself," the older woman said with a mysterious smile. "You stay here with Shannon. The moonlight is beautiful tonight. Perfect for a walk around the property."

Before either Parker or Shannon could protest, Aunt Shirley had whisked his mother away, leaving them alone in the softly lit great room.

"I think we've been set up," Shannon observed, her voice carrying gentle amusement.

"Thoroughly," Parker agreed. He pulled Shannon closer, savoring the quiet intimacy of being alone together after such an emotionally intense day.

"I've decided I'm not sorry, after all," Shannon said

suddenly, the words tumbling out. "For calling the cops on you that first day."

Parker blinked, taken aback by the abrupt change of subject. "Oh? I'm not sure how to take that."

She laughed, and the sound sent warmth through his chest. "What I mean is, if I hadn't made that mistake, I might never have tried so hard to make things right with you. I might never have gotten to know you, might never have seen past the surface to who you really are underneath." She shifted to face him more fully, her hands finding his. "And I'm so glad that I know you. That I love you."

Wonder filled Parker's heart as understanding dawned. "You're saying our worst beginning led to our best relationship."

"I'm saying God can use even our mistakes to bring us exactly where we need to be," she replied, her voice carrying complete certainty. "That first day was humiliating and painful for both of us. But it also forced us to really see each other, to work through assumptions and fears and old wounds."

Parker studied her face in the firelight, memorizing the way her eyes sparkled with unshed tears, the gentle curve of her mouth, the trust written in every line of her expression.

"What are you planning to do with the money your mom saved?" Shannon asked softly.

His heart hammered against his ribs as he gathered the courage to voice what he'd been thinking about. "I thought we could use it for a house." He paused, letting the weight of his implication settle between them. "Shannon, I'm hoping that someday, you'll be ready to trust me with your heart. Always. Not just for now, not just until something better comes along, but for the rest of our lives."

He watched her closely, seeing when his meaning fully registered. Her eyes widened, then softened with something that looked like joy mixed with certainty.

"Parker," she said, her voice steady despite the tears

threatening to spill over. "I have another confession."

"Hmm?"

"I might be ready for forever sooner than you think."

His heart soared as he leaned down to kiss her, tasting apple pie and new beginnings and a love he'd never dared to hope for. Whatever came next, they'd face it together. After all, they made a great team.

From the Author

THANKS FOR WALKING with Parker and Shannon through their journey of love, forgiveness, and healing.

I'll be honest, twins in romance sometimes make me roll my eyes. But for years, I couldn't shake this story. The meet-cute played on repeat in my mind, refusing to let go until I finally wrote it down exactly as I'd always envisioned it.

I thought I was writing a straightforward love story where a woman falls for the identical twin of a man who shattered her heart years earlier. Simple enough, right? Woman meets Twin A, gets betrayed. Woman unknowingly meets Twin B, sparks fly, complications ensue.

Except that's not what happened at all.

As I dove into that explosive meet-cute I'd been planning for years, I realized this story demanded so much more. The question that sparked my creativity was: How does a woman move from painful betrayal, through the shock of mistaking Parker for his criminal twin, to genuinely falling in love with Parker himself?

That's when the deeper themes revealed themselves. This isn't just a mistaken identity. It's about forgiveness at the deepest level—for both Parker and Shannon. It's about confronting the brokenness from their childhoods and the lies they've believed about themselves. These wounds created rich soil for God to work in their hearts, for forgiveness to take root, and for love to bloom in unexpected ways.

What surprised me most was Parker's character arc. I spent weeks brainstorming what it must be like to be the identical twin of such an awful man. How would that shape his view of himself? His place in his family? His relationships with his mom, his dad, even his twin? What emotional wounds would he carry? And what if Parker was a Christmas Eve Christian, someone who kept God at arm's length because of his hardships?

Could landing a job at Vargas Ranch, surrounded by men of deep faith like Dylan and Adan, change the course of his life?

These questions led me to places I didn't expect. Parker became one of my most complex heroes, and Shannon's journey toward trust became one of my favorite heroine arcs. I hope this story reminded you that healing is possible, even when the past shows up wearing a familiar face.

What's Next for Love at Vargas Ranch?

Cole Gregory has been carrying an engagement ring for six months, but he can't seem to propose to Sydney Steele. Five almost-proposals later, Sydney reaches her breaking point on her thirtieth birthday. Cole must finally confront the secret from his past that's been paralyzing him—or lose the woman he loves.

Continue their story in Book 2: *Her Almost Fiancé Cowboy*.

Karen Baney

Read Cole & Sydney's story

About the Author

Karen Baney is passionate about writing stories full of flawed characters. She enjoys weaving together stories of second chances, redemption, and overcoming personal trials. As a transplant to Arizona, she loves researching the state's history and finding ways to seamlessly incorporate real history and real settings into her novels. In addition to writing and speaking, Karen works as a Software Development Manager for a Christian ministry.

Her faith plays an important role both in her life and in her writing. Karen and her husband, Jim, make their home in Gilbert, Arizona, with their two dogs, Bella and Daisy. Both Jim and Karen are active at Rock Point Church in Queen Creek, Arizona.

Discover faith-laced stories with characters who feel like lifelong friends.

Visit www.karenbaney.com to discover more historical romance series set in the American West. Follow Karen's writing journey and get behind-the-scenes glimpses of her research adventures on social media.

Facebook: @AuthorKarenBaney
X: @karen_baney
Instagram: @AuthorKarenBaney
BookBub: Follow Karen Baney for new release alerts

Books By Karen Baney

<u>Contemporary Romance</u>

<u>Vargas Ranch Series:</u>
Love is in the air at the Vargas Guest Ranch & Resort near Wickenburg, Arizona. Meet the Vargas family—five swoon-worthy brothers and their cousins who live by their family motto: "We do not deviate from the Lord's plan." These rugged cowboys run a successful working ranch and luxury resort while navigating the rollercoaster of finding true love.

Falling for a Fake Cowboy
Falling for a Real Cowboy
Honeymoon with a Real Cowboy
Falling for a Shy Cowboy
Falling for a Bossy Cowboy
Falling for a Smart Cowboy
Falling for a Humbug Cowboy
Falling for a Devoted Cowgirl
Falling for a Pregnant Cowgirl
Falling for a Cowboy's Legacy

<u>Love at Vargas Ranch Series</u>
At a sprawling guest ranch near Wickenburg, Arizona, the series follows the hearts of hardworking cowboys, wranglers, and staff who keep the ranch alive. From equine therapy programs to trail rides under endless desert skies, each story brings together two wounded hearts longing for healing, hope, and love.

Her Mistaken Identity Cowboy
Her Almost Fiancé Cowboy
Her Brave Rookie Cowboy

Her Valentines Veteran Cowboy
More books planned

Steadfast Love Series:
The *Steadfast Love* series follows a close-knit group of friends as they navigate the beautiful mess of modern life in the Phoenix area—workplace drama, complicated families, and love that shows up when they least expect it. These contemporary romances blend emotional depth with authentic faith, reminding us that even when life unravels, God's love never does.

The Heart I Rescue (prequel)
The Air I Breathe

Historical Western Romance

Prescott Pioneers Series:
Step back in time to the wild, untamed Arizona Territory where survival depends on grit, faith, and the courage to start over. Follow three pioneer families—the Andersons, Colters, and Larsons—as they risk everything for the promise of a new life in a land that demands both strength and hope.

A Dream Unfolding
A Heart Renewed
A Life Restored
A Hope Revealed
Hidden Prospects

Desert Manna Series:
Sometimes the most beautiful love stories bloom in the desert. Set in the growing frontier town of Prescott during the early 1870s, these tender romances follow women rebuilding their lives after heartbreak and the unexpected men who

help them discover that second chances at love are worth the risk. Set in Prescott, Arizona between 1871 - 1873.

Beauty for Ashes
Joy for Mourning
Oaks of Justice

Colter Sons Series:
Power, legacy, and forbidden love collide in this sweeping family saga set in the Arizona Territory. The Colter ranch empire has weathered decades of frontier life, but now family secrets and buried betrayals threaten to destroy everything. As five brothers—and one resilient sister—navigate the treacherous waters of love, loss, and redemption, they must decide what's worth fighting for. Set in Prescott and other locations within the Arizona Territory in 1887 - 1906.

The Reluctant Cattleman
The Roaming Adventurer
The Railroad Magnate
The Resourceful Stockman
The Restless Wrangler
The Resilient Bride

Larson Sisters Series
Meet the next generation! These delightful novellas follow the three daughters of Adam and Julia Larson from the *Prescott Pioneers Series* as they navigate love, courtship, and finding their own happily ever afters in territorial Arizona in 1886 – 1894.

In Love at Christmas
In Love with the Rancher
In Love with the Horse Trainer

Desert Life Media

———

Desert Life Media: *There Is Life in The Desert*

Entertainment-first Christian fiction set in the Southwest, featuring redemption, family, and faith

Publishing clean, wholesome, and uplifting fiction since 2010

———

desertlifemedia.com

www.ingramcontent.com/pod-product-compliance
Lightning Source LLC
Chambersburg PA
CBHW060918250626
47159CB00008B/3067